Steam Over Stephensport

Also by Carolyn Bond
- Bluegrass Blush
  (Steam Through Time - Book One)
- Between Time

i

Steam Over Stephensport

Steam Through Time Series

Book Two

By Carolyn Bond

Published by Timepiece Books. Lexington, Kentucky, USA

ISBN-13: 978-1724082862

Carolyn Bond would love to hear from you if you enjoyed this book. Follow her web page at www.carolynbondwriter.com or email her at carolynbondwriter@yahoo.com.

Acknowledgements

I want to thank my husband Jeff for being my own example of "a man that will always love me." The love he has shown, by not just affection or kindness, but with passion and a servant heart, has carried me through several very hard situations while writing this book. While Lily and Evan's relationship is uniquely their own, as a writer I draw on my emotions to weave the words. Having a wonderful relationship with Jeff gives me a treasure chest of emotions to draw from.

Thank you to my mother and father, Ashley and Larry Trautner, who taught me to dream and to persevere. Those two things are the most magical tools we have and they can change lives.

I would also like to thank my editor, Dr. Beth Case. She has taken my work to a new level and I can't thank her enough. Nancy Griffin's editing helped me reach a personal goal of having this book accepted by the 2018 Kentucky Book Fair, and for that, I am so grateful. Thank you to Valerie Brock, one of my beta readers, who gives me insights that I would never have imagined. And thank you to the ladies of Susannah Hart Shelby Chapter, NSDAR. You are all faithful, encouraging friends whom I love and admire.

This book is dedicated to all the women in the history of our country that imagined more and didn't give up.

Part I

Chapter 1 – 2018

Craning her neck to see what used to be the old Black's Farm, Lily looked at Sinking Creek as it disappeared in the leafless trees. Being in a place where her ancestors had lived out their lives, she had a feeling of peace and connectedness. It was just what she needed. In her own life, she'd come untied from the lines that secured her to the harbor of family and now floated helplessly with the current of her emotion. In a distracted moment, she visualized herself lost in rough water.

The car jolted unexpectedly as the wheels hit the concrete curb. Pulling her eyes away from the hushed landscape, she barely saw the front edge of the metal bridge before it tore into her driver's side bumper with a groaning scrape of metal. The car was suddenly airborne. Her stomach floated in her abdomen with sickening levity. She couldn't see where the car was headed but she knew it was going toward the creek below.

She froze as the burn of adrenaline coursed through her arms to her finger tips.

"Oh no!" she mouthed. She closed her eyes and waited for the impact. Time seemed to stop.

"It's taking too long," she whispered with her eyes shut tight.

The sound of running water trickling past the side of the car crept into her senses. She blinked open her eyes and held her breath. The car sat on the edge of the creek, half in the water. It reminded her of a nightmare where she was too scared of getting shot, so she never felt the gunshot, but suddenly blood covered your shirt.

"I didn't feel the impact," she said out loud as though surely angels must be seeing this.

Water pooled at her feet and she felt the car slipping in the mud as the current pushed it farther toward the mouth of the creek. Beyond that, she knew the mighty Ohio would wash it away and it would sink to the dark, muddy bottom. She had to move fast while the car was still bobbing on the surface. The river's current was nothing to mess around with.

She opened the door and water rushed in around her legs as the car sank faster. The car turned backwards as the current pushed against the fin-like doors. She flung herself out into the creek just as the car was pulled down, nose diving for the bottom, the trunk barely showing above the water.

She made her way to the edge by swimming parallel to the current. Muddy brown water swirled around her. She could taste dirt in her mouth but it was oddly easier to move in the water than she expected.

"*Don't panic. Just keep swimming,*" she told herself.

She reached, caught the trunk of a small tree and pulled herself half out of the water. Her feet slid on the mud as she tried to get a foothold.

She turned just in time to see the last of her car slide under the muddy, churning crests of river water just beyond the place where Sinking Creek dumped into the Ohio. A sob rose and threatened to choke her.

3

"My car!" The burning rush of adrenaline still pumped repeatedly out to her hands and feet. Her teeth began to chatter. She had to get out of the water before shock set in. Her dress hung loosely from her shoulders as though it had been stretched in the water.

The sunlight dimmed as a cloud passed in front of the winter sun. She heard a ringing vibration and winced at the pain in her ears. Her arms looked strange, thinner and her skin smoother. She held her hand out in front of her. Her freckles were gone. Not that she was a very freckly person before, but now there were none. She squinted and rubbed the mud from the top of her arm. The humming sound grew louder as the pressure in her head increased to an unbearable level.

All sound and light left her in that brief instance. She fell back and landed on the soft dead grass of the bank. A rush of exhale left her lips before darkness consumed her vision.

***

Earlier that morning

"I just don't think this relationship is going to work out."

The words clanged in her mind like a deafening bell. After all the time they had been together.

He kept talking but she could only watch his lips move. All sound stopped while the repeating phrase clogged her brain.

"...don't think this relationship is going to work out."

"It's not you. It's me. I just can't commit the way you want me to and I feel bad about it."

Her mind raced through jumbles of comebacks but none made clear sense. "But, but don't you love me? How can you want to split?" She regretted saying it as soon as the desperate words fell from her mouth.

His eyes darted away as his mouth pressed together. He sighed and turned back pleading, "Don't you see? I don't want to hurt you anymore. This isn't good for either of us. I do care about you, but I can't marry you and I know marriage is what you want."

"But," her sentence cut off as she realized there was no going back this time. They had broken up a few times before, but this time he sounded different.

"Lily, its better this way," he said softly.

"But we can be friends, right?"

He shook his head. "It would only make it harder." He paused a minute and shifted his weight as though trying to fight a decision. "I'm going to leave now. I have to work early today." He turned his back to her, took a step and half turned back, but stopped himself. Then in a rush of determination, he left her standing alone in her kitchen. She heard the soft click of the front door closing.

Her throat constricted as a lump rose. Hot tears welled and fell down her cheeks. Five years of hoping he would fall in love with her, hoping he would see that he couldn't live without her, came to an end.

"Five years wasted!"

She balled her hands into fists and squeezed as hard as she could.

"How could he do this to me?" she thought. *"I've been everything he needed. I gave him my whole heart. I was the only one that really understood him. And now, he just decides we can't even be friends!"*

"Jerk!" she spat out through her gritted teeth. A burning roil of molten lead grew in her stomach. She looked around the apartment and memories of the times they shared played like overlapping movies. Her mind numbed and only the stillness surrounded her. She walked over to the window and pulled back the curtain. She scanned the parking spaces near the walkway at the base of her stairs. His car was already gone. She dashed a tear off her cheek and let go of a sob.

Rubbing her eyes, she noticed a landscaper working in a flowerbed near the mailboxes. "*January is an odd time for gardening,*" she thought. His straw hat covered his face but what caught her eye was the tender way he held the branches as he trimmed away last year's growth. He stopped, frozen momentarily, and slowly turned his gaze up to her window.

She wanted to jump back, but her feet were rooted to the ground. He looked at her with such sadness.

"What's this guy's story?" she wondered. She quickly pulled the curtain closed but still could not move. She could make out his shape through the fabric. He slowly turned back and kept working on the bush.

"I'm super-imposing my broken heart on other people." She turned and looked around the lifeless room. "I have to get out of here."

***

The bare trees reflected the empty feeling gripping her. The cut, white limestone rose in statuesque walls along the sides of the desolate Bluegrass Parkway. She looked at the tree-covered, rocky landscape as her ancestors must have seen it. Time felt like layers of alternating shuffled cards. Her timeline and theirs touched. She imagined her great-grandparents traveling beside her in a wagon. She felt their comforting presence.

She flipped through the radio stations. She was too far from any major city to get the music stations. Angry preachers yelled through her car speakers with bursts of emotion.

"You can find everything you ever dreamed of inside the doors of a church. If you never go, you will never know. Hellfire awaits those who refuse to see the truth. This very day January 2nd, of the year 2018, follow your heart. It knows what's true!"

She pressed the volume button to silence the assault. The last thing she needed to hear was their intrusive ranting like some turn-of-the-century revival sermon. Silence surrounded her, giving her space to be alone with her thoughts. The two-hour drive to Stephensport to talk to her grandmother was just what she needed. She needed to figure out how she felt. Other than a pounding pulse, she couldn't describe the intense emotions flooding her brain. It was all white noise in her head.

Every mile took Lily farther from the pain and the pressure that surrounded her at home in Frankfort. Andrew had dumped her, but it felt like so much more than that.

The loss of Andrew's companionship left her adrift. He was more than a boyfriend, he'd become her best friend. Nearly every day for five years they'd talked all day by text and email at work. They called each other every night and talked until they went to bed in their separate homes. She thought back to the countless festivals and movies, or touristy things they had done together. Andrew was safe to her. His Baptist church was safe. Follow the rules and you know your soul is fine. Dating him was the same way. As long as she avoided his pet peeves and didn't pry too much into his past, he gave her all the attention she needed. While he seemed to enjoy her company, it never translated into the love she was looking for. She kept telling herself that, in time, he would see that he couldn't live without her. She'd invested in this relationship so heavily that she really didn't have any other friends.

Maybe she had made him into a super hero that would rescue her from becoming an old maid. At thirty-six, her options were running thin. He said that he couldn't be what she needed. Her forehead scrunched together: what did she need? She wasn't even sure what that was. She just didn't want to be alone. A string of failed relationships littered her love resume'.

Granted, he wasn't perfect, but he made her feel like she was somebody. She had auditioned for the part of his wife for a long time. She had it down. Apparently he just really didn't want a wife. But, she couldn't shake the nagging question, why didn't he love her? Was there something about her despite what he said?

Tears streamed down her cheeks. The ache in her heart felt like a weight that sucked the air out of her lungs. The road blurred in her vision and she smeared away the tears in a fit of anger. She blamed herself for being so stupid. She'd let herself be a doormat. She knew the relationship had issues within the first few months but brushed them off. He just needed time to trust again, she thought. Whatever his problem was, she decided, it was his. She told herself she was a good person: giving, pretty and intelligent. She had a nurturing personality and put others' needs ahead of her own. She was an experienced fourth grade teacher. She was a capable leader and could take care of herself. She'd won awards for her teaching and leadership. What's more, she didn't need Andrew's authoritarian religion meddling in her life, either, with their weekly Sunday school lessons telling her what she could and couldn't do.

After he left that morning and she was alone in her apartment, she decided she had to get away from Frankfort. She just had to be by herself to think. She loved visiting her grandmother's grave at Cedar Hill Cemetery in Stephensport along the Ohio River. A sudden heart attack took her grandmother away. She always felt like she and her grandmother were connected. After she passed, Lily could still feel her spirit on that grassy hill overlooking the quiet Ohio. She couldn't wait to sit under the shade tree and feel the river breeze tousle her hair. It was so serene and otherworldly.

She'd pulled a clean, white cotton dress over her head and hastily packed an overnight bag. She gave herself a glance in the mirror by the door. A gray hair was woven into her waves of auburn hair near her temple. She reached up and pulled the solitary reminder that she wasn't getting any younger. With her coffee in hand, she was ready to burn up the roads. The landscaper was gone by the time she bounded down the steps in her white sneakers. She knew she was acting on defense mechanisms but she didn't care. She didn't even tell her parents where she was going. She figured she would find a roadside hotel to stay the night and have a personal retreat. As an only child, she knew they would worry, so she resolved to call them as soon as she checked in somewhere.

Her mind shifted back to reality when the enormous road signs for the Leitchfield exit came into view. As the sun was gaining intensity, she turned off the Parkway. This was the final leg of the journey. The two-lane country roads were so far off the beaten path that a stranger would get lost. She remembered the first time she'd set out to make her way to the cemetery alone. She crisscrossed rolling Kentucky farmland and tiny roads lined with tall trees for hours. They all looked the same until, by a stroke of luck, she found the hidden metal bridge over Sinking Creek at the edge of the tiny town of Stephensport.

It was not much of a town to speak of. One short road that traversed about 200 yards from the bridge to the base of Cedar Hill sitting on the sleepy bank of the wide Ohio River. You could catch glimpses of the gently flowing river between houses on the right side of the road. Sinking Creek had a wide mouth that emptied into the river after appearing out of the trees of a bend. Her mom had warned her long ago to be careful of the creek where it empties into the Ohio. The current of the Ohio was strong and pulled anything in the creek into its depths. The banks of the creek were muddy and not much to see but she felt like it was home. The house where her great-grandfather lived still stood by the bank. It was now deserted and overgrown with weeds. Ghosts of generations before him rustled dried grass and bare winter branches of maple trees. This was her land, even though her grandparents had moved away when her mother was a baby. She could hear the whispers of love on the gentle breeze.

About a dozen or so houses lined the quiet passage through the small hamlet. An old church with stained glass windows and a large shady lawn and a plain little building for a post office were the only public establishments. If you blinked twice, you'd miss the whole town and find yourself crossing a railroad track before the main road veered off to the left. Right there, though, a non-descript one-lane paved drive kept going straight from town before disappearing in some cedar trees at the base of a good size hill.

Lily pulled the steering wheel to the left to follow the narrow road as it wound up the hill. Giving her Toyota Camry a little gas to fight gravity on the narrow incline, the sleepy cemetery came into view. Hundreds of headstones covered the upward slope and disappeared over the crest of the hill. A black, wrought iron sign with the words "Cedar Hill Cemetery" traversed the entrance.

Each season here had its own feel. She loved coming in the spring, summer and fall. The winter, though, had an eerie feeling. It felt like the dead were sleeping and she had come to visit too early, before it was polite. She could imagine the spirits lazily looking up to see who had disturbed their slumber as she walked up the solitary road, crunching the thin layer of gravel.

Next to an old tree casting jagged shadows across the ground, Nanette Black's granite stone came into view. Lily made her way over the brown dormant grass, being careful not to step right in front of any headstones where she knew a coffin lay underneath. It just seemed rude to step on a grave. Reaching her grandmother's final resting spot, she finally spread a small lap blanket on the hard ground to sit on. She pulled her knees up against herself and hugged them. Closing her eyes, she let her head drop back as she looked up into the evergreen tree's dense mash of branches. She took a deep breath and opened her eyes. The crystal winter sky was a blue so deep you could almost make out the darkness of space behind the atmosphere.

Returning her focus to the earth beneath her, she relaxed into a cross-legged pose with her feet tucked under the knee-length hem of her dress. She studied the etched letters on the stone, tracing them with her fingertips. A soft wind picked up the edges of her loose blond hair causing the roots to stand on end and giving her an unexpected shiver. Despite being the only living person on the hill, she no longer felt alone.

It always happened here. She felt a caress on her shoulder that could have been a touch or a soft wind. She looked around to be sure, but as she expected, no one else was visiting the cemetery.

"Grandma, I know you're here. I'm glad. I miss you." She paused, thinking, before starting again, "You know that guy I was seeing? Andrew? Well, he broke up with me. I guess it's for the best. He says he never loved me. I," she hesitated. "I thought he did." She scrunched her brows trying to understand how she could have been so wrong.

Lily could imagine her grandmother's expression. *"I would have told him, 'Good riddance!'"* Lily could hear the words ring in her head as clear as day.

She continued, "I know there will be others, but I've already given my heart to a man who didn't love me and look where I am now. What if Andrew had married me?" She paused, "I know what he wanted. I tried to be that person. He wanted a nice wife. I could be a nice wife." Flicking away the fallen pale blue berries from the cedar tree on the ground beside her, "I just also want to change the world one child at a time. Lots of them. Whole classes full of them. Is that why he didn't love me? Because I wanted more than just him?"

She sighed, picked up a sprig of cedar that was on the ground beside her and twirled it in her fingers. The strong woody scent tickled her nose.

"Grandma, I wish I could hear what you have to say about it. If you can, help me find the man who would love me with all of his heart."

She rested in the quiet company of souls who couldn't speak to her, but she knew sat with her in her sadness. The greenery in the cedar tree, with tiny blue berry-like cones, had always been her favorite for making Christmas garland. Holding it next to her nose, she took a deep breath and let out a sigh. Using a rhinestone-encrusted pin she had in her

12

hair, she secured a sprig and fastened it back to hold her shaggy bangs out of her face.

Chapter 2 – Black's Farm 1889

She felt a tapping on her cheek and heard a gentle man's pleading, "Lass, are you well? Lass?"

Her mind swirled without catching on any coherent thought. She felt the cold that had permeated from the ground into her back. Her body convulsed in a shiver. The fabric of her dress clung to her with wet heaviness.

"Where am I? What happened? My car?" The words never left her mouth but rolled in her head.

Reality pulled at her like a magnet insisting she leave the dream world she was lost in and her eyes fluttered open. She had been pulled up into a semi reclining position by an arm that felt like a hot oak tree branch. She focused on the face of the man attached to the arm, which was only a few inches from her. His eyes seemed familiar, as though she knew him, but she couldn't think of his name. His velvety Scottish accent rolled off his tongue.

"There you go, lass! Come on, now! I dinna want to startle you."

"Did I wake up in Scotland?" she thought to herself.

He was coaxing her toward consciousness. Before she could clearly make out his features, her body was already reacting to him. Warmth grew in the deep pit of her belly like a smoldering fire. The world stopped spinning and her eyes connected to his. In the same instant, the fire in her belly coursed through her insides, lit up every nerve in her spine, and settled into a pulsating flash under the base of her skull. She was not injured. This was passion she had not felt in a long time.

She drank in his gaze and in the space of three seconds, determined no man had ever affected her so quickly. Jet black hair, loose and wild, framed a swarthy face with a short growth of dark facial hair. She found herself staring into eyes that were the uncanny likeness of the sky over Cedar Hill: that deep celestial blue that hints of a universe hidden behind it. She had no control over her wandering gaze that drifted down his face to lips that she yearned to feel on hers.

Regaining her composure, she pushed herself up to a sitting position. From this upright position, she could see his odd clothes: a natural colored, plain tunic over a pair of darker trousers and boots that almost had a handmade look about them. He wore no watch or other jewelry. He watched her looking him over and leaned back proudly as if pleased with the attention.

"Do you like what you see, lass?" chuckling.

"What?" she answered.

"Well, it's no every day a bonny lass affords me such attention," he smiled broadly.

She blushed and darted her eyes away, "What? What happened? My car! Did you see my car? Did I pass out?"

She turned her gaze back the creek looking for her car and then stood up, ignoring his confused expression. She stumbled from rock to rock to get a better view of the mouth of the creek. A small envelope floated past on the water. It was the envelope with the money she got out at the bank that morning. Bending at the waist, she splashed around with her hand in the silty creek mud to draw it toward her but it zipped by undeterred from its path toward the choppy river. She heard him clear his throat and jerked around to see what was bothering him. She sighed in frustration now that her money was gone with her car.

He had turned his head and partially covered his eyes to block his view of her.

"What? What's the matter?"

He nearly choked on his words, "Lass, you're in your chemise. Where is your dress? Were you bathing? In that dirty river?" The last question was strained.

"What?" She was getting frustrated with this odd talking man, even if his dialect did make her stomach float like a butterfly. "What are you talking about? This *is* my dress."

"Ach! Well then. You'll be needing a covering, lass, unless you want to be hauled off by the sheriff for indecency."

"Huh?" her mouth fell open as she quickly examined her dress front and back, twisting this way and that. The only thing wrong was that it seemed a size too large for her now.

"Mind you, you're a right bonny lass, despite the mud and bits of tree in your flaxen hair, but that much leg you only see on a wee bairn."

"A what? You aren't making any sense. Didn't you see my car go over the bridge and into the creek? Who are you, anyway?"

"The name's Evan. Evan McEwen. And nay, I did not see anything fall from the bridge. What is this *kargh* that you speak of?"

She raised her hand to shield her eyes from the midday sun and squinted as she looked again. The bridge was a simple wood bridge, not the caterpillar-like gray metal bridge with arched supports.

"What? What happened to it? That's not the bridge. But," her voice trailed off. She turned back to look him over. "What do you mean 'what is a car?'"

"I have never heard of such a thing. If you describe it, I'd be happy to help you search for it among the rocks." He started to move small rocks around with the toe of his boot.

The shock was easing but her frustration was growing. None of this made sense. She clenched her fists and started walking up the bank. Maybe with a better view, she thought, she would be able to figure this out. Something tickled her mind. Something he said was bugging her but she couldn't remember what it was. Then it hit her: flaxen hair. She reached up and grabbed a handful of hair and pulled it around to her face to look at it.

She gasped. Long blond hair. Her short sassy auburn hair was now very long and as fair as vanilla ice cream.

"Miss, uh, you shouldn't be about dressed like that. Let me help you get home. What's your name? Where're your people?"

"What in the world?" she muttered about her hair. Then realizing her asked her a question, "I am Lily Black Wallingsford. And *my people* live far away from here."

"Black? You said Black?"

She turned to face him. "Yes. Do you understand English? Where are you from?"

"Ay, lass, I understand English fine. I'm a Scotsman. I only asked to be sure. Ye're sitting on Black's farm, so how can yer people be far away? Perhaps ye hit yer heid and now you're confounded."

He stood up and started walking toward her shielding his view of her from the neck down with the back of his hand.

With his hand raised, she thought he was about to strike her. "What are you doing? Get back!"

"Lass, I'm afraid yer boggled in the heid."

"I'm not boggled, whatever that is!"

"What else would a sensible person think finding you lying passed out in a creek wearing yer sark and not knowing you were on your own people's land?"

"My *people* haven't lived here for nearly fifty years since the last of them passed away. I have no idea who lives here now."

"That so, huh?" He looked into her eyes questioningly.

"Yes! My great-grandfather was the last to live here as an old man. I'm not even sure when he passed but I think it may have been before my mother was even born."

"And who was your great grand pappy?"

"Carlton Black"

"Carlton," he turned away and scratched his head. "What about Bettie and William Black? Are they your kin?"

"Bettie? Ye mean Sarah Elizabeth?"

"Yes, Bettie."

"Well, Sarah Elizabeth and William Black were Carlton's parents. Way back in the 1800s."

"*Way* back, eh?"

"Yes. Why are you smirking at me?"

"It's just you say you didn't hit your bonny head, but you don't seem to know what century you're in. Another thing is that little Carlton couldn't be a great-grandpappy. He is only eight years old. If I add that into the rest of the odd things about you, I'd say you were a downright loon."

"What?" She put her hands on her hips. "I didn't hit my head. I nearly drowned. You must be talking about some other family. Like I said, my family is gone from here now. They have been since Carlton died, probably in the 1960s." Her fingers crawled across her hips to her belly of their own accord and she looked down at them. She pressed the fabric against her skin and pressed her forehead into a wrinkled mess. Her waist was now firm and small enough that she could nearly touch fingertips around herself. Her jaw fell open as she tried to take in this new fact.

"I don't think this is my body," she mumbled to herself. "Is this some kind of crazy dream?"

He stopped then and stared at her steadily.

"Lass, perhaps ye better come in and get a bite to eat. I'm worried about ye. Yer talking crazy." He raised his hand to stop her and looked around. Thinking better, he said, "Bide here."

He disappeared behind the bluff of the creek and returned shortly with a sheet.

"I'm worried about me, too," she mumbled to herself. She pulled a lock of now damp blond hair around to her face. Even her fingers didn't look like hers. They were more delicate. She reached up to her face with both hands and felt like she were blind. It was not her face. Soft, young, supple cheeks met her finger tips. Her mouth was much smaller than her wide grin. She ran her hands over her bosom and froze. Looking down at her ample hourglass figure, it was no wonder the man acted so oddly.

"This was hanging on the line, so it's still a bit damp, but it'll cover you to get inside without causing a spectacle."

She hoped this was not some sort of prudish fundamentalist religious farm, but for the sake of modesty, she pulled the sheet around her shoulders. She hadn't heard anyone use the word 'spectacle' like that since her grandmother Nanette was alive.

***

Earlier, Evan was heading to the creek to blow off some steam. It was all he could do to walk away without landing his fist in Brian Everbright's hooked nose. The muscle in his

19

right arm twitched as he flexed his fingers. The man raised Evan's hackles by just standing there. Brian was the son of a merchant who had a department store in Stephensport. The store modeled itself as an emporium for the needs of a proper estate. Complete with ready-made house staff uniforms, you could sail in right off the Belle of the Ohio and pick up everything a dignified home would need.

The store was not the problem in Evan's mind. If people of means wanted to spend their money frivolously, that was their business. However, he could do without Brian Everbright's sour puss look of contempt, as though Evan just standing next to him would sully his waistcoat.

Brian had been walking down Main Street when Evan turned to leave the blacksmith's shop. The Black's fool ox had managed to pull apart two links of chain on the plow when it hit a limestone slab. Evan thought the animal was so stubborn it would rather tear the plow apart than give in to solid rock. Evan said goodbye to Mr. Ames in the shop and collided into Brian.

Evan had been plowing all morning and had a good layer of dust from head to toe. Brian made a disgusted groan and began slapping his black jacket to send the offending earth flying. After the confused outburst subsided, he looked up to determine the source of his sudden dust bath and the muscles of his cheeks simultaneously scrunched upward while his brows pressed down causing his eyes to narrow to tiny slits.

Evan suppressed the urge to laugh out loud. The scene in front of him was comical. You would be hard pressed not to assume Brian had been attacked by fire ants from the way he danced around. Then with the sudden change of countenance ending in a glare, Evan found himself checking his features for deadpan expression so as to not light the fuse and have Brian explode. The bottled up fury was palpable.

He was about to apologize out of courtesy, but then Brian did it. He went too far. He stepped forward and thrust his finger up in Evan's face. Growling out the words, his venomous hatred let loose.

"Evan McEwen, you don't know your place in this town. Since you are new, I'll give you a lesson. Your filth is a disgrace. Maybe in whatever backwards hovel you came from there were no civilized gentlemen, but here you will have to learn to respect the class of men that make Stephensport the fine city that it is. Left to scum like yourself, this town would be nothing but a muck-filled river swamp knee-deep in sludge, just like you. Now you will work very hard to make sure I never get close enough to you that your filth could touch me. Am I clear, Hillbilly dog?"

With the word 'dog', Brian gave Evan a two-handed shove before turning his shoulder away and setting off up the sidewalk with his chin jutted in the air. Evan had been the object of scorn before, being an immigrant, but this was the first time someone had cut him so low. The bile rose in his throat as he thought back to all he had endured just to get to America. Brian Everbright had no idea and Evan was certain Brian's mamby-pamby wimpiness would never have let him survive the same journey. He watched Brian march away like a dictator and the sting of truth hit him like arrows with acid tips. His family in Scotland had several descendants of Billy Boys who'd supported King William in his defeat of King James II. Now here in America, any Scotsman was labeled a Hillbilly for their differentness.

Any pride one had for their convictions, for being known as a Billy Boy, was stripped away here. Billy Boy had turned to Hillbilly and its connotation of ignorance. Brian would never understand the bravery of being a Billy Boy and opposing the sitting king and what's more, he didn't care. This was America. The land with no kings. The land where you could make yourself a king if you were smart enough. The colonialists in America saw only their own history as valuable and whatever respect Evan had in Scotland was gone here.

***

Lily glanced behind her as she walked. The man seemed lost in thought. They made their way up the bank and across a narrow strip of harvested farmland. The cool clumps of dirt crunched as she stepped across the rows in her sneakers. Decaying foliage lay in withered frost-bitten layers. Not being a country girl in the least, she couldn't figure out what crop that must have yielded. The back of a red brick two-story home could be seen hidden behind a thicket of skeletal bushes and leafless trees. She slowed as they came to the clearing between the trees and the house. The big farmhouse was just as she had imagined a few minutes before when she was walking up the creek. She turned back to him seeking assurance. The whole ordeal about her drastic body changes, her apparently inappropriate dress and the sheet had her worried. If he thought she looked out of place, who knew what the occupants of this home would think. She had the urge to just run back to the creek and bridge. Surely her car was somewhere close. None of this made sense.

"What ails ye? Get on, now. Ye canna be seen out like that."

There was no reasoning with him. She'd just let him lead her to whatever destination he seemed to think would help her and then she would get out there as fast as she could. As they approached the back of the house, the door flung open and a panful of water flew through the air in a silvery streak with steam rising off its back as it flew. Lily jumped to avoid being hit.

"Laws a'mighty, Evan! Sneaking up on me like that, you nearly got scalded! And who is this?"

A short tiny woman in a full-length black Victorian dress complete with high neck and lace around her wrists stood in front of them with her hands on her hips. Lily didn't see her move her legs but somehow the spry young woman seems to have flown down the steps and appeared within inches of her. Her chestnut brown hair was pulled tightly back into a bun with rings of curls framing her face. Though she had no make-up on, her porcelain skin contrasted with the burst of rose on her cheeks and lips.

"Bettie, this is a lass I found lying out on the creek bank. She seems to be lacking her gown. I thought you'd be able to tend to her."

Bettie looked Lily up and down as she circled around her, "Well, now. What have we here? Were you assaulted, girl?"

"Uh," she stammered, "no. I nearly drowned when my car crashed into the creek."

"Hm! Your kargh, you say?" Bettie had a puzzled look on her face. "Perhaps your gown got pulled off in the water, then. Well get inside before you catch your death of cold fanning around like that. Evan, there's some ham biscuits on the table. Get yourself something to eat while I tend to our guest."

Bettie took her by the hand and led her into the house. Despite the fact that she looked much younger, Bettie acted at least ten years more mature than Lily felt. They didn't say a word until they got all the way upstairs and Bettie closed her bedroom door.

"Chil', what are you doing out and about like that? Are you ill?" Bettie turned around to face her and then scanned her clothes.

"I, I don't know, exactly. What's wrong with my dress?"

"What's wrong? What's wrong?" Bettie stammered like she didn't understand the question.

"Yes. And why are you in that get-up? Is this a historic home where you give tours?"

Bettie's eyes went wide, "Historic home? Tours? No, child. This is my home. My husband's and my home, and our son's. Get-up? I am up."

"This makes no sense." Lily rubbed her eyes and the coolness of her finger tips felt wonderful seeping through her eyelids. With her eyes closed and no sound, she could imagine none of this was happening.

"Darlin', I am going to let you borrow one of my gowns until we can figure out what happened to you. I suspect you fell and hit your head on a rock. Do you have any sore spots on your head? I would say you have been the victim of an attempted bamboozle. At least, I hope it's just 'attempted'. Whatever the case, we will find your people. Surely they are desperate to find you right now. You're too pretty to be a heathen. Someone must be looking for you."

"A heathen?" she thought to herself. There was a word she had not heard since she was a little girl. She tried to remember just what it meant. Was it someone who was not a Christian or just someone who was trashy, she couldn't remember the context in which her mother had used it.

Bettie opened a door to a very shallow closet. Two dresses hung on a nail facing outward. Lily pushed back the thought that these were all the clothes this woman had: the dress on her back and two in a closet. Surely there had to be more somewhere. She scanned the room. There was another closet like this one, but she was certain it was of the same dimensions. A man's antique shaving set with a cup and water pitcher was on the bureau. The other closet had to be for his clothes. Her mind darted to her own deep walk-in closet full of hundreds of shirts, skirts, pants and dresses.

The realization that somehow she must be in the past was settling on her. There was no explanation for it, but there was no other way to explain Bettie and Evan's reactions, clothes, or world. The metal bridge was gone. This house looked like a working museum. None of them seemed to be actors. And what was the deal about her body? She never looked like this. She seemed much younger and smaller. Maybe she was dreaming and would wake up soon. Whatever the case, she tried to just go with the flow.

Bettie handed her a long black dress. Lily noticed the delicate poofs at the shoulder seam and the flair of the fabric that tapered down to the wrist. Layers of lace and ruffles were hand sewn on the bodice and back of the skirt. Bettie patted Lily's waist and gasped.

"Were you pulled right from your bed? You don't even have on a corset!"

"A corset? Why would I have on a corset?"

Bettie threw up her hands and chuckled. "I agree, darling. Why do we wear those things?"

She pulled open a drawer of a high boy chest of drawers and produced a strappy, boney piece of lingerie. She told Lily to raise her arms and she pulled it over her head and down below Lily's bust right over her white dress which was dry now, but still had mud in places. Despite being unlaced, it already pinched her hips and cut into the soft skin of her sides.

Bettie turned her around and started pulling on the laces from the bottom, tightening as she went up. "Suck in your

25

breath, for heaven's sake. And, I don't believe I have ever seen shoes quite like that."

Lily looked down at her sneakers and didn't know what to say. She took a breath and let it out, allowing her diaphragm to pull in her belly as Bettie tugged the laces tighter and tighter. Holding her breath for so long caused blackness to cloud the edges of her vision. Tiny stars of light pricked her eyesight.

With puffs of exhaled air being the only sounds of life she could make, Bettie tied the strings off. Lily inhaled in short, chest-raising breaths. Her hand reflexively went to her waist and she furrowed her brow. She tried to look but her bosom was now pushed upward to such an extreme it was like the top of a loaf of bread. This gave muffin-top a whole new meaning that no one in the 21st century would have thought of. She stifled a giggle as she thought of what Bettie would think of the 2018 image of a muffin top.

Holding up a strange looking belt with a giant egg-shaped pillow sewn on, Bettie said, "I'm sorry this is all I have. It's a little out of date now but, well, a natural form bustle is the best I can afford."

The block of sculpted padding rested on her back side. Next, she threw the black dress over her head and smoothed it down around her waist. Lily reached into the sleeves until her hands popped out the other end. The cuff around the wrist was quite constricting. She had to fight the urge to rip the dress off her. Bettie started buttoning the line of tiny buttons up the back and the dress molded to her now exceedingly feminine shape.

Bettie turned her around and looked her up and down, "It's a tad bit small on you, but not by much. At least the skirt is long enough to cover your shoes. Can you put your hair up or do you need help?"

"Put my hair up?"

"Well yes, unless you want people to think you're a saloon girl!" she laughed out loud.

At this point, Lily resigned to do whatever she was told. "Sure. Do you have some pins?"

"Of course, darlin'. Have a seat at the vanity and you'll find anything you need. If you don't mind, just come downstairs when you're finished. I need to tend to the rest of dinner."

"Bettie, thank you. Thank you for helping me."

Bettie's face lit up with a huge smile, "Of course, honey. What else would I do?"

She turned and left, clicking the door closed as she passed through. Lily turned to the vanity. She sat on the small stool and slowly took in the reflection. A stranger looked back. Lily saw beautiful young woman with delicate bones and messy long blond hair dressed in a plain but very feminine gown. The stranger eyed her fearfully, like she was going to run away at any moment. How could this reflection be her? She raised her arm to run her fingers through the damp mop of long hair. Even with dirt from the river, the waving rivulets glowed like threads of gold. A small widow's peak hair line gave her face a heart-shaped form.

"Who was this person? How did I end up in this body?" she wondered. She touched the unfamiliar face with her fingertips. "Where did the occupant of this body go and where is my body?" Did she drown in the creek in the future, she wondered?

A horse hair brush with a silver handle lay in front of her. The initials SEA were engraved in the smooth dome encircled by scrolls of acanthus leaves. It seemed like an awfully nice hairbrush for a lady who can't seem to afford the latest fashions.

27

The initials SEA circled her mind. *How pretty, like the ocean.* Then it hit her: *Sarah Elizabeth Avitt!* This was her great, great grandmother! She jumped to her feet and dizziness washed from her head to her legs. Darkness threatened to close in as her mind reeled. She stumbled backwards and tripped, landing on the bed. The lump of padded block pressed against the small of her back. She held up the brush again and examined it.

Light from the window gleamed along the edge of the back of the brush. In large etched scrolling letters, the initials were as clear as day. The brush was in perfect condition, as though it were lovingly polished every day. The large A in the middle stood majestically proclaiming a family whom Sarah was now tenuously connected to. She remembered the story. Her mother had told her many times. Sarah Elizabeth married for love. She went against her father's wishes. He turned his back on her and told her if she married the poor farmer, she would live a farmer's life.

This brush was what she'd brought from her father's house when she got married. How long ago was that, she wondered? The man said Carlton was a boy. It must have been eight or ten years before. That's why she had the older fashioned bustle. It was probably the height of fashion when she married.

"Never you mind, sweet Sarah Elizabeth, bustles are about to go out of fashion altogether," Lily thought.

She gazed absent mindedly toward the door where Bettie had gone out. Without realizing she had been holding her breath, she felt light headed again. Prickles of light pierced her vision. She pulled open the drawer of the vanity looking for anything to give her a clue. A small sheet of paper with a curled corner ruffled in the air of the quick action. She pulled it out to read it and gasped as panic seized her. It was a handwritten receipt for fabric complete with the store name and the date.

"Oh, Lord, help me. This is 1889."

Truth hit her with paralyzing force. It was all true. The strange man with his comments about her clothes. Bettie's comments about her hair being down and questions of being assaulted. This 'historical' home. The dress with the corset she was wearing.

This was her ancestor, just a few generations down from Captain Thomas Helm, her Revolutionary War ancestor that she and her mother had declared on their application to the Daughters of the American Revolution. She thought about the ladies at the Susannah Hart Shelby chapter in Frankfort. What would they think of this? When she got back to her own time, she could do quite a thorough historical presentation at the next meeting. She wondered if Bettie was in the DAR. How great would it be to attend a meeting here in this time?

This time?

"But how am I here? Who am I here?" the words escaped out loud. "And how can I get back? I can't stay here."

At least it was winter break and she was off work. The day before she had never been so pleased to wish her students a merry Christmas and pack them into cars and school buses with candy canes and baggies of candy from their gift exchange.

Those children, they haven't been born yet. And with more horror she realized, *I have not been born yet.*

She sucked in a breath and clutched her stomach to hold back a wave of nausea. Reality was not setting well in her head. She could feel the stiff fabric and bones of the corset holding her abdomen hostage. She stood up and waited a moment for her head to stop spinning, then tiptoed to the door. Grateful she still had her sneakers on underneath her dress.

She turned the cold metal door knob and peeked down the hall. The upstairs was quiet. She made her way to the steps and quietly stole down, watching for someone to jump in front of her. Maybe she could slip away, she thought. If she could get back somehow, she would feel so much better. She didn't belong here and her stomach was letting her know that as it rolled in panic. She had no idea what she could tell them; certainly not the truth.

She stepped out the front door onto a wide porch. A long dirt road stretched before her before disappearing into a line of trees. She could hear the sounds of carriages and men shouting in the distance. She was close to town. It was so much louder than in 2018. Looking back into the parlor one last time, she regretted not having more time to speak with Bettie, but she had to get away. Closing the door with a quiet click, she dashed for the dirt road and made it to the tree line in seconds flat.

Chapter 3 – Stephensport of the Past

As she emerged from the trees on the other side, she stopped cold. This was not Stephensport. It was a different town. Logic made her mind reel as she tried to make sense of it. She had just driven down Main Street a few hours before. Granted, that was over a hundred years from now, but generally, in her experience, when you have been away from a town and come back in the future, there are new buildings and the roads are wider and more crowded. This made no sense.

In 2018, there was one two-lane road down the middle of Main Street with a small metal building for a post office and maybe a dozen houses. That might be exaggerating, she laughed to herself. The scene in front of her was sobering, yet made her feel slap-happy as well. It was the same length as Main Street 2018: maybe 200 yards. However, two-story buildings lined both sides of the road. The road itself was a patchwork of flat limestone rocks nestled together perfectly. The hooves of horses clopped along on the stones pulling carriages and wagons.

A wide sidewalk of the same stone was sectioned off the main road by a border of raised rounded rock.

The glass shop windows displayed ladies ruffled gowns made of silk and men's dress wear that made any tuxedo she

31

had ever seen look dull. Other windows displayed furniture and dishes. A silversmith had a display of tea services and buffet dishes.

With her eyes about to pop out of her head, she jumped and nearly fell when the crack of a steam-wheeler's horn on the river let loose. The blaring dirge announced its presence. Immediately, a dozen or so men in dusty work clothes exited a saloon door with loud cackles and laughter. One looked her way and immediately whistled.

"I'll be back soon. Wait for me, angel!" He motioned with a tilt of his head back toward the saloon.

Her jaw dropped, appalled at his cat call, and her eyes traveled over the front of the saloon. The upstairs windows had velvet curtains with ball fringe. A sign on the front brazenly invited anyone to "Wet your whistle and have some company." There was an image of man in a formal black suit with a woman leaning on his shoulders. She was wearing a short dress and was kicking her leg out. With one hand she was flipping her loose hair while she laughed garishly.

Lily instinctively reached up to touch her loose hair. She'd darted from the house before putting her hair up as Bettie suggested. Horrified, she twisted it and held it up against the back of her head. She needed a bobby pin. Surely someone had lost one, she thought, as she looked around the ground in front of her. She darted to the boardwalk and discreetly started looking for anything that would hold her hair up. She didn't find anything remotely like a bobby pin, but she did find what she recognized as a hat pin. It was about an eight-inch long straight pin with an ornate metal medallion encircling a pearl on the end. No doubt, it was dislodged from a hat in a gust of wind.

She looked the long needle wondering if she could wrap her hair around it and tuck it under like she used to make a pencil bun on hot days in the classroom. It had been years since she had long hair, but she thought she could make this work. Careful to not poke herself, she twisted her hair around the shaft working it down to the point. She then twisted the pin behind and out to secure it next to her scalp. It certainly wasn't as fancy as the women walking around town had their hair but at least it was up.

She looked into each of the windows mesmerized by the luxuriously formal wares. Everything looked like the town was expecting the queen of England to come shopping. She wondered who bought this stuff. The townspeople, she noticed, were dressed like the mannequins in silk and wool with perfectly styled hair. Their overcoats had grosgrain and silk ribbon trim. Men wore top hats. Horse-drawn carriages clopped by with silk curtains framing faces that looked like royalty. The girls had ringlet curls and furs trimming their cloaks.

The winter air wasn't terribly cold but it seemed they wore them more to show off than to keep warm. She thought perhaps people had come to town to shop. Oddly, though, she didn't feel the shopping vibe from these people. It felt more like they were conducting their own private parades.

Her attention was caught by a man's voice across the road. She turned to see a young man come out of Everbright's Fine Home Mercantile. His dark oiled hair perfectly contrasted with his pale skin and yet matched the dark color of his suit. He was shaking hands with a lady and her husband as they were going in and welcoming them and a pang of jealously gripped her. Something about this man ensnared her. She wanted to feel his touch on her hand in a most primal way despite the fact that he was complete stranger. Like finally meeting your soul mate, the one your mother would have spoken of for years, she felt a pull to him that she could not deny. If ever there was a real Prince Charming that would rescue her from every unpleasant facet of life, it had to be him. His sweet smile radiated to his eyes as he ushered them inside with an offer of warm cider. To her, it sounded like an invitation to come home. She stumbled forward a step toward the store, toward this man, when she halted as he turned his head in her direction.

Like a person feeling the gaze of another, his gray-blue eyes shifted to her as the couple passed in front of him. He gave her a head-to-toe assessment and she could detect a hungry look of desire as his eyes opened wider, but then he just smiled politely before ducking in behind the couple. She felt slighted in a way. It was as though she didn't pass the muster. She looked down at her gown and realized that was it, of course. This gown was Bettie's out-of-date fashion. She knew she had looks that could get attention if she wanted it. This body was her dream come true, better than any diet she had ever been on. With renewed confidence, she straightened and started walking away from him along the stone sidewalk. She stole a peak back at him under her dark lashes curious if he looked back.

He did, and again they briefly locked eyes. He pressed his lips together and turned his back to her as he strode into the store. His brush off left her feeling like she had swallowed sour milk, so she kept moving down the stone walkway. It's not like she was looking for a date, but that was not the response she expected. The startling rush of heat surprised her. He was entirely appealing with a genteel beauty and gentleman courtesy toward the shoppers. He charmed them and she felt it, too. However, the class difference was real and apparently not to be overcome. She shrugged it off and tried to ignore her jangled emotions. It was rare that man affected her like that and it bothered her. She never wanted to be a slave to lust.

Near the end of the town, before the railroad tracks intersected Main Street and veered to the left away from the river, Lily saw a sign that said, "Cedar Hill Cemetery" with an arrow pointing toward a dirt road. Her heart leapt at the familiar sight.

Being distracted as she was, she didn't see a group of teenagers on the other side of the tracks smoking cigarettes. They saw her immediately and started whispering to each other. A tall lanky young man straightened and patted down his shirt, checking to make sure it was tucked in. He tossed the half-smoked cigarette into the bushes and winked at the young man next to him.

"Miss? Miss? Can I help you?" he asked as he approached.

Lily turned and looked him up and down and then noticed his friends back on the side of the tracks. "No. I don't need any help." She tried to sound stern.

He smiled an oily grin and stepped closer. "Now, miss. Surely you ain't out and about alone? Something could happen." He stood very still like a tiger ready to strike.

The hairs on the back of her neck stood on end. "Leave me alone!" She turned and headed up the dirt road to the cemetery. Her error struck her immediately. She was now moving farther away from town and people. The road turned a corner and bushes obstructed the view. She sucked in a breath. If she turned around, she would head right back into the group of boys but if she kept going she would be even more alone.

In the split second she tried to figure out what to do, it was decided for her. The group of four boys casually walked up behind her. The tall lanky boy was on her in a flash holding her around the waist with an iron grip. For such a young man, he was as strong as a python.

His mouth was on her ear as he breathed in. "Oh my, miss, but you do smell nice."

"Let me go!" she yelled and tried to stomp on his foot. If she could just remember the self-defense moves she had learned once.

The other boys laughed a low growling chuckle and one said, "Save some for me now! Don't get her all dirty before I get my chance!"

Horror struck her. This was a nightmare. She wasn't that far from town, just fifty yards maybe. It was broad daylight.

She had to alert someone. If she could just get someone's attention, maybe they would run. The lanky boy was now hiking up her skirt and running his calloused hand up her thigh. In a surge of primal provocation, she made a fist and jerked her right elbow back with all the force she had. It worked. She made contact with his ribs and he jerked at the pain, momentarily letting go of her. She picked up her skirts and put her Nike running shoes to the test. A train whistled and the breath left her. It was a few yards away on the track. Pulling out her high school track team moves, she did a running long jump just as it curved around the edge of town. The boys had been chasing her but were cut off by the train. She turned as the train passed, panting, and saw her attackers were blocked. She darted into the post office to hide.

Hiding out of view, she watched the train pass and her assailants search Main Street with their eyes for her. The tall boy rubbed his rib cage. She knew it could only be a bruise. She wasn't strong enough to break a bone. One of them made a face and slugged him in the shoulder. He gestured back with his hands and the group of them made their way up the tracks in the direction the train came from.

She waited a good fifteen minutes and then cautiously darted back up the road to the cemetery. It made no sense, but the only safe place she could think of was with her grandma. She just wanted to feel her grandma's presence.

She ran up the one-lane dirt path that wound up the steep hill. She was gasping for air by the time she got to the cemetery. She wished she could rip the corset right out from under her dress. Standing finally without gasping for breath, she scanned the rising hillside just past the sign.

It looked altogether different. There were headstones to the right of the road that passed through the arched sign. They looked vaguely familiar. There were no other headstones. She glanced to where her grandmother should be buried. Nothing there. It was just a gentle rolling slope of grass. She jogged under the arched entrance and up the hill to the height of Cedar Hill. From here the cemetery should continue downward in the direction of the Ohio River for about fifty more yards. Through the leafless trees, she could make out the silent movement of the river current as it slinked its way to the west. There were no graves back here though. The only graves were in the front and on the right side.

Tracing the landscape in her mind, she made her way to the virgin ground where her grandmother would someday be buried. A small seedling had pushed its way through the tall grass and had a good start before hibernating for winter. She fell to her knees and caressed its twig-like trunk. Was this the same tree? Had time wound backward so far that towering trees were seedlings and cemeteries were nearly barren? It was true then. She really had traveled back in time. How, she had no idea. She thought back to when she met Even at the creek. What happened before then? Rubbing her temples, she remembered the jolt that sent her flying. Pressing her mind backward, she felt the jolt when her wheel hit the curb. Then there was nothing for too long. Like time stopped.

There was no answer. Then she remembered the ringing sound and blacking out on the creek side. Other than not paying attention to the road, she couldn't think of anything she had done. Maybe it wasn't her. Maybe someone else did this and she was a part of their plan. She glanced back to the untouched earth of her grandmother's grave.

Was she to blame for this? Had her grandmother done this? Would it be possible?

She didn't feel her grandmother's spirit here like she did before. Of course that would make sense. Her grandmother hadn't been born, yet.

"What am I supposed to do now?" she yelled.

She couldn't decide if she was yelling at her grandmother or God. She finally decided it must have been God. After all, her grandmother didn't exist, yet. Tears sprang to her eyes and she dashed them away angrily.

"Only you, God, could bend time. This must be your will!" She spat out, "Well I don't like it. Take me home!"

With legs pulled up, she clasped her arms and hugged her knees and cried with everything in her. The rushing of her pulse in her ears blocked all sound. She felt utterly alone. At least before she could come to her grandmother's grave and have her one-way conversations. Now, even that was gone.

When all the grief had poured out of her and all that was left was numbness, she looked up over her clasped wrists. Evan sat cross-legged in front of her waiting. He watched her without saying a word. A sad but serious demeanor held his expression.

"Are you done cursing God, lass? Looks like he whooped you pretty good for it."

She stared at him trying to figure out what he meant. He chuckled at her and stood up, offering his hand to help her up. She stared at it.

What was he doing here? Did he follow her? She looked into his warm eyes and felt safe. He seemed to genuinely care about her. Surely he must think she is crazy. Especially if he heard her conversation with God. She took his hand finally, and let him pull her to her feet.

"Did you follow me?"

"Bettie and I thought you'd been gone a while and went looking for you. When we couldn't find you, we got worried. I ran into town just in time to see you heading up here."

She imagined him and Bettie searching the house. Why would they care that a stranger disappeared? She meant nothing to them.

"I see," she said distantly. "But Evan, why did you bother? You don't know me. In fact, you probably think I'm crazy."

He looked down at his feet and chuckled again. When he looked back in her eyes, she felt like she could see straight into his soul. His eyes weren't flat, but rather like staring into history playing out in front of you with emotions swirling through it.

"Miss Wallingsford, I bothered because I cannot bear to see you hurt. You have no one to care for you. At least, I suppose, until we find your people."

"I don't need anyone caring for me! I'm not a child."

He let out a heavy breath of frustration, "Nay, miss, I can see with my own eyes you're no' a child. You must be careful, though."

She furrowed her brows.

"Surely, you won't argue with me about guarding your virtue!"

She didn't see how her virtue was in any jeopardy. Then, the cat calls from the man leaving the saloon echoed in her ear. Perhaps he was right. They thought about things differently here. The notion of a prim 1950s school girl reputation was not what he was talking about. This was more a matter of being assaulted and then having people say it was your own fault. If you had no one to protect you, in their eyes, it was your own fault.

She inhaled and released it slowly in resignation. Seeing it through his eyes, he wasn't treating her like a child. He was protecting her from opportunists.

"Thank you, Evan. That was kind of you."

He shifted his weight and stood a bit straighter, accepting her compliment. "But, Miss Wallingsford, it's not that I don't like it, but it's not proper for you to call me by my given name. People will talk. Perhaps that is different where you come from, then."

"Ah. No. You're right, Mr. McEwen. Pardon me," she paused, "familiarity."

His lips stretched into a flirty smirk, "Perhaps one day, you'll find me familiar enough to resume. I can only hope."

Heat engulfed her face and her arms and legs felt like disjointed and stiff as she walked. To break the awkwardness, she tried to think of conversation.

"Mr. McEwen, is Stephensport a dangerous town for women?"

"Not especially. However, with the river and the train, there is a fair amount of people passing through. It would be wise to be prudent. A lass as yourself would do well not to go about unchaperoned. If for no other reason than just to keep away uninvited unpleasantness."

"I see."

Before they turned the corner to Main Street, he stopped as though he'd forgotten something, "Miss Wallingsford, not that I was trying to eavesdrop on your, um, conversation with God, but what did you mean about God bending time?"

Fear caught her. Surely she couldn't tell him the truth. He would think she was crazy. "What do you mean?"

"Just that. I heard you plain as day." The wind picked up the dry brown leaves on the ground and swirled them around their feet. "I ask because, where I come from, witches are nothing to mess with."

The laugh burst out before she could stop it, "Me! A witch? Mercy, no!"

"Then what, pray tell, were you discussing with the Almighty?"

"Don't you think that is rather my business?"

"Certainly. However, if you are going to be bring all sorts of spooks and haunts on Mrs. Black's house, then I have a right to ask."

She tried to think of what to say, "Mr. McEwen, something happened to me. I didn't cause it. I don't know what did. I can't explain it. I will tell you, since you have been kind to me and offered me your protection, I am not from here. I am from far away. I am not even sure if I can ever get back."

He took her hand in his and pulled it to his soft warm lips. A surge of energy twisted her insides in a most delicious way.

After a brief kiss on her knuckles, he said, "That makes two of us then. I certainly won't hold that against you."

She felt such peace because he was so easy to be with. He accepted her vague answer and didn't pressure her. What's more, he identified with her. He held out his arm as an invitation and she took it, looping her hand under his bicep and over his forearm. No man her age had ever offered his arm like this. Maybe as they walked into prom in high school, but never as a man would offer his protection. As she looked down the length of Main Street stretched out before them, she felt like the whole world fell away and knelt down before her. She felt like royalty, riding on Evan McEwen's coattails.

Her moment of majesty crashed as quickly as it came, though, when she saw the look on the face of the man in the Fine Clothes Mercantile. It didn't matter what year it was because the look meant the same thing in any time. She hadn't noticed the hook shape of his nose before. It was much easier to see now that he was staring down it at them with half-closed lids. She could feel an itchy filthiness creep up her arms in reaction to his scowl.

Evan whispered under his breath, "Pay him no mind, Miss Wallingsford. His house is of glass, made by his own hands. It must tire him to be without fault all the time."

Her mouth still puckered in confusion over the school-boy display of snobbery, she nodded and turned her eyes toward the small church to their right. A girl who could not have been a day over fourteen slammed the door and stomped down the steps. Lily had seen that look before. It was exasperation. She had seen it on the faces of her friends who worked in the schools. It was the pent up rage and fatigue of someone who had given their whole heart and gotten a slap on the face. It happened frequently to teachers.

The girl hurried down the walk and disappeared around a corner, passing a small wood sign identifying the church as the "Stephensport Common School." A tickle of intrigue piqued her interest. How could that girl have been a teacher? She was too young.

Evan turned the corner and the bustle of Main Street faded behind the cover of brush that lined the narrow dirt road. In the unfettered peace of a country estate, her thoughts drifted back to Evan. He walked beside her without speaking, seemingly lost in thought. She stole a glance to her left to see that his brows were knitted together and his jaw worked a clinched muscle in his cheek.

As they walked towards Bettie's home, the house had a welcoming look with a red front door under a wide porch. The white clapboard siding and ornate wood trim glowed pristine in the afternoon sun. Black shutters couched windows upstairs and down.

Four rocking chairs beckoned her to rest and sit a spell. A globe oil lamp in the front window reflected the afternoon light and gave the appearance that the house had a light of its own. There was depth of life in this house. It was the light and soul that came from the collective unity of the people that called it home.

The front door swung wide with a burst. Standing there like the lord of the manner, a little boy of about eight years old sized her up and gave her a grin. He marched down the stairs toward her without letting her eyes go. In all her years teaching fourth grade, she had seen a few young men with such charisma. They were a rare breed. While they gave her all the respect of her position, they acted completely as her equal. He stopped in front of her and waited for her to get a good look.

"Miss Wallingsford, I presume?" he asked as he reached for her hand.

Without thinking, she extended her right hand forward to shake his hand. He didn't move but looked at her hand and a chuckle burst from his lips.

"You're an odd girl."

Unsure of what he meant, she looked at Evan for explanation.

"You offered your hand as a man does. I think he is not sure how to proceed."

"Oh. Sorry for the confusion. Is this better?"

She rotated her thumb under to offer the back of her hand in a more demure salutation.

The boy took it and gave her a kiss that felt like soft wind on a fall day, then, "May I introduce myself? I am Carlton Black."

She froze. The edge of her vision blurred tunneling in on the face of the boy in front of her. A boy who was her great-great-grandfather. A boy who died before she was born. He died an old man. The image of a photograph appeared in her mind. An elderly man with a long pointed white beard super-imposed itself over the boy's face. The blurred edges of her vision closed in even further until his eyes were the only thing clear. Same eyes.

Stomach acid rose until it burned in her throat as nausea threatened to overtake her. Her hands slid over her hips until her fingers touched and she pressed in hoping to secure her suddenly wavering insides. Her mind cramped and stretched to get around what she knew was reality and what stood before her.

"Carlton?"

"Yes, ma'am." He tilted his head ever so slightly trying to understand the panic in her eyes. "Would you care to rest? There is a chair."

He motioned toward the rocking chair.

"Miss Wallingsford? You look like you've had a fright. Bide here." Evan gently pressed his hand against the small of her back.

The ground seemed to shift as she stepped up onto the porch. She struggled to remain upright. She felt an arm encircle her waist. The heat of the soft side of his arm seared through her dress distracting her from the reality dilemma. She leaned into the safe hollow under his arm against his chest. Letting go of her panic, she closed her eyes and let him lead her to the chair.

"Sit here, Miss Wallingsford. Carlton, get her a glass of water."

"Yes, sir." He dashed into the house through the front door.

Evan knelt on one knee in front of her, "Are you well? What's ailing you?"

"It's just," she broke off not knowing how to explain it. "I don't," she tried again. "Carlton," was all she could manage to say.

"At the creek you told me. You told me you had a great-great-grandpap named Carlton. Miss Wallingsford, is he," he paused. "Do you think he is the same person? Is it possible?"

She locked on his eyes. "Yes," she breathed.

He grimaced without breaking the gaze they shared. "Are you saying--"

"How can it be?" she interrupted.

He sighed and paused before answering, "So, you would be from the future, then? Is it really true?"

"I suppose so. How is that even possible? I mean, I'm just me. I was driving. It was 2018 and then," she trailed off thinking how she wasn't really herself, either, but she couldn't tell him that. "I don't remember anything

45

particularly earth shattering happening. Shouldn't I have felt something?"

"You're asking me?" He stared at her incredulously.

"So, you believe me?"

"I have to admit you don't act like any woman I have ever met. You do seem very genuine in your reactions. Either you are telling the truth or you are truly insane."

The front door creaked as Carlton burst through with a sloshing glass of water. "Here Miss Wallingsford. You alright, ma'am?"

His chocolate-colored brown eyes were wide with concern.

"What's going on out here?" Bettie belted out as the door creaked swinging wide. With a bang, it slammed back just as she flew to Lily's side.

"I just got a bit dizzy, I think. I'm fine."

Bettie looked her up and down quickly and crossed her arms. "When's the last time you ate, darling?"

"Ate? Oh my." She thought about breakfast. Of course that was a century ago. Or, would it not be for another century? She was lost in her thoughts.

"You must be delirious." Turning to Evan, "Get her inside, Mr. McEwen."

Evan took her hand and reached under her arm with the other hand. Lily felt herself hoisted up out of the chair. Bettie got under her other arm and she was unceremoniously led and then deposited into a chair on the kitchen table.

The table had already been set with rolls and a glass pitcher of water. The glass had small air bubbles trapped in it making it look like a frozen wave. A teapot and three teacups waited next to the water pitcher. Bettie ladled thick stew into three small white china bowls and carried them on a wood tray to the table.

"Well let's tend to our belly and then things will seem clearer." She winked at Lily.

"It smells delicious!" Lily said.

"Just regular old stew, but thanks. Mr. McEwen, where did you find her?"

"She was up at the cemetery."

Bettie looked at her. "Do you have family up there, darling?"

"I, well, I thought I did."

"Who are you looking for?" Bettie placed a bowl at each setting.

"My grandmother." Lily bit back a pang of grief that twisted her insides.

Bettie sat down and reached her hands out on both sides palm up. "Shall we give thanks?"

They all held hands while she prayed, "We thank thee, our heavenly Father, for the sustenance your hand provides. Amen."

"Amen," said the others.

Bettie looked at them and waved her hand encouraging them to dig in.

Lily spooned a bite of broth drenched potato in her mouth and couldn't stop the moan of satisfaction. "This is so good! I guess I *am* hungry, after all."

Bettie smiled warmly accepting the compliment. "So who are your people, darlin? Do we know them?"

Lily coughed to stall, "I, uh, well, I am related to you through Thomas Helm."

Bettie stopped and pursed her lips looking at her with her head tilted. "Huh. Are you from George's line?"

Lily's eyebrows perked up. "Yes! So that makes me a distant cousin."

Bettie looked at her closely and then exclaimed, "We are so glad to have you! Mr. McEwen, how fortunate you came across her before anything unseemly happened."

"Rightly so. That was fortunate. There are many strangers that come through town. It's not safe for a woman alone."

"So where are you from, Lily?" said Bettie.

"My parents and I live in Frankfort."

"Frankfort! Well that's not far. In fact, we have had several relatives with business in Frankfort. Did you travel alone?"

"Yes, no. Well, I traveled with a friend but she went on to Owensboro. So no. That would be crazy, right?" Lily felt a rising flush of heat creep up her neck. She hated lying but didn't know how to explain what would be thought of as bizarre behavior. Bettie and Evan were giving her a stone-faced stare as they were evidently trying to make sense of her. Bettie broke the awkward moment by turning toward her bowl and spooning another bite of stew into her mouth. Evan just continued to study her before giving her a reassuring upturn of one corner of his mouth. She hoped this meant he could be trusted.

"Bettie, I was wondering, in Frankfort I'm a member of DAR. Are you? Do you have a chapter here?"

Bettie studied her intently before answering, "Darlin, what in the world is the DAR?"

"Daughters of the American Revolution?" she offered.

"No, ma'am. I've never heard of them. What do they do?"

"It's a patriotic society."

"I see. Well, ever since that Colonial Exposition back in '76, there have been a great many of those spring up."

A pang of shock hit Lily. Maybe the DAR hadn't been founded yet. She couldn't remember exactly when it was founded. She didn't know what to say next.

Bettie jumped in before she had to, "No matter that I haven't heard of it. I have been busy here since I married William. Before then, mother and I used to be involved in several groups. There was a woman, Mary Desha, I think, in Lexington that's a teacher. Mother was in the same social circles and we would see her occasionally. She was always quite vocal about us ladies persevering in educating others about our country's history and helping our community in the name of patriotism. I think it's a good idea. I think I heard she is in Alaska now teaching the natives and fed up with how Washington isn't doing anything to help those people."

Lily remembered a presentation at a chapter meeting about Mary Desha. Mary Desha was one of the organizing members of the National Society, Daughters of the American Revolution. The year 1890 came to mind.

Whoops! No wonder Bettie has no idea what I'm talking about.

Changing the subject, Lily said, "So where is Mr. Black?"

Bettie took the change well and relaxed her shoulders, "Oh, Mr. Black, yes, he has gone to meet with the town council members. Seems we need to find a new teacher for the school. Apparently the last one got all in a huff and told the council members she would never teach their-, let's see, how did she say it? Yes, I've got it: Their wee bastard primates! Apparently one of the boys said she wasn't fit to polish his shoes. He's a surly uppity boy, but then again, this poor girl couldn't have been a day over fourteen. She and he were nearly the same age."

"Fourteen! The teacher was just fourteen?" said Lily.

"I agree. Fourteen is just too young. The teacher should at least be sixteen," said Bettie.

"Sixteen? You're kidding me. Surely they should at least be through high school."

"Through high school? We would never find a teacher at all if we required that."

Lily thought for a moment. She remembered learning about the one-room school houses prior to the legislation that created public schools. She knew they were mostly headed by single women. She remembered a funny article on Facebook about the requirements of teachers around 1900. They had to be single and not drink, be chaste, and other crazy things modern companies could never require of an employee. She tried to imagine these teachers as fourteen year olds. Surely not. Then again, girls would get married as young as sixteen or eighteen. At thirty-six, she was an old maid by their standards. She looked at the smooth firm skin on her hands and wondered how old she was in this body. If she had to guess, she must have been about twenty-one.

She wondered if she should mention she was teacher. She didn't know how long she would be here. She wasn't even sure how to get back. Maybe she was stuck here. A pang clenched her gut and she reflexively pulled her hand up to her stomach.

"Are you alright, dear? Does the stew not suit you?"

"Oh, no. I'm not sick. Just thinking."

Evan watched her as though taking note of her every move. She glanced up to double check the feeling of being watched and found him solidly contemplating her. Her belly lurched again, but this time in a delightful way. A warm rush flushed her neck again and she suppressed a girlish giggle but could not stop the sudden curve of her lips as she turned away.

Apparently pleased with his effect on her, his face changed to a subtle grin. He picked up his spoon and sipped the warm broth.

"Just what are you thinking about, then?" he asked still grinning.

Bettie noticed his puffed up countenance and raised her brows.

Lily raised her eyes to him and tried to cover the quiver inside her, "I was just thinking that I am a trained teacher and perhaps I could help out until a new teacher is found."

Bettie, startled by this revelation, turned to her and gasped, "Really? That would be wonderful! I know the town council would be so pleased. We have such a hard time finding good teachers with experience." Then she scowled at her stew, "The last three have been worthless, mamby-pamby things. Carlton doesn't help the problem. He makes their time here difficult. He seems to like you, though."

"Carlton? He goes to school there?" Then she caught herself. "Well, of course he does. Maybe he could give me some pointers about things others have tried that didn't work."

"Perhaps. He is a smart boy. However, I can tell you what you need. A firm hand will go far. The uppity children act like they are too good to take orders and the farm children are out as often as they are there. It surely must make it difficult to teach any of them anything."

Uppity well-to-do kids were nothing new to her. She had taught at an affluent public school. She knew there were definite rewards to teaching children of parents of means. She often had volunteers and never ran short of supplies. A good communication line also meant she could get parents to help students with homework.

Farm children being absent frequently was a different problem. She was used to poorer children being absent due to the transient nature of their lives and lack of transportation to school. She had an idea, this was going to be a different problem, though. While the farmers were most likely poorer, they were likely not as transient and could walk to school. There was no way to fight harvest season.

"I'd be happy to fill in for the time being. I can't guarantee how long since I'll have to go back home at some point."

Lily noticed Evan's face took on a dark cast.

"I'm certain that any time you could give the school would be appreciated. You will be staying here with us, won't you?" asked Bettie.

She hadn't even thought about where she would be staying. She didn't have any money. She didn't even have any clothes. Grateful for the offer, she said, "Oh, Mrs. Black, it would be so kind of you to let me stay here. Thank you."

"Certainly, darling! You're family. But you must call me Bettie."

Lily was very pleased. How odd, she thought, to be in her great-great-great grandmother's house and soon to be teacher of her great-great-grandfather.

"Carlton!" Bettie hollered out. Carlton came skipping into the kitchen.

"Yes, ma'am?"

"Carlton, sweetie, run in to town and go to the town hall building. Tell your daddy I have a teacher for him that can start right away. Go straight there, you hear me?"

His face contorted into a frown. "Yes, ma'am," he grumbled before darting off. They heard the screen door slam in his wake.

Bettie winked at Lily and then said, "Now they won't pay you hardly anything but you will get a little something for your trouble."

"Does the school have books? Does the town council make the curriculum?"

Bettie and Even exchanged glances. "No dear. You will need to do all that. Did they do that where you taught before?" Bettie asked.

"Well, yes, the school board was very strict about exactly what the children must learn."

"Hm. I would say just teach what you have taught before. As far as the town council is concerned, they follow what the church tells them should be taught."

That worried Lily. Men at a church deciding the direction of education, supposedly basing it on what they thought the Bible wanted them to do. That could be good or really bad. The 19th century wasn't known for busting out of convention. Convention had women dressed up to their chin and down to their toes. Convention made people stay in line with strict class lines where the poor did not rub elbows with the aristocracy. Convention also made people put on a face for society that was more about show than a reflection of their true character.

They finished their meal and Bettie cleared the table.

"Lily, I need to go upstairs and freshen up your room. Would you excuse me?"

"Certainly, but you don't have to go to any trouble for me."

"Oh, no trouble dear. I just want to put out some fresh linens. Make yourself comfortable and I'll be back in a jiffy." She paused and then turned to Evan, "And you behave yourself, Mr. McEwen." She winked at Lily as she turned away.

Lily gave Evan a wary smile.

"No need to worry, Miss Wallingford. I'm quite house trained, despite Mrs. Black's admonition." He smirked.

"So what is your story, Mr. McEwen?"

"My story? Well, I stay here with the Blacks. William hired me on about a year ago. I came from Scotland to find a new life. Some of my clan settled up river a ways and I started there, but took a job on a paddle wheeler and found my way here. I liked it here. The soil is so good. The land is lush and green, rich soil, and, well, William needed a farm hand."

"I see. Was it hard? Leaving Scotland? Coming somewhere unknown and being alone?"

His gaze drifted out the window while he thought of an answer, "In some ways. I miss my family. But, there was nothing for me there. Being the third son, I had no land, no home of my own." He turned to her. "Here, I can work as my strength allows and create my own legacy. There is freedom here to make my way. In Scotland, everything goes to my older brother. My sisters go to their husband's land. I would never have my own land. I would always be a farmhand on my brother's lands."

The concept was hard for Lily to get her head around. "Never? You would always be a farmhand? Why couldn't you get your own land?"

"All the land is passed down based upon your birth order. Unless my two older brothers died, I have no land of my own. It is a good system for keeping the estate whole."

"I see. That makes sense. But-- it's so unfair to you."

54

"Yes and no. There are responsibilities for being the laird that I would not have to deal with. The laird takes care of several families. And, I would always be taken care of. I had a cottage to live in. As long as I gave my allegiance to the laird, I shared in the food and supplies."

"But that didn't' sound like a good life to you?"

"It is good. It's not that I'm not grateful." He looked down at his hands. "I just want to make my own life. Besides, my brother is a bit hard headed and difficult to live with." He smiled as he told her this.

"That seems reasonable, that you wanted to have your own life. Every person should be able to choose what they want."

He turned his head to the side and sucked in his breath quietly. She barely heard the whooshing sound as his diaphragm contracted. There was no mistaking the lusty wistful look in his eye.

"I agree, lass. Sometimes we have to look on the other side of the world to find what we want." The corners of his mouth turned up.

"Mr. McEwen, are you flirting with me?" She leveled an assertive gaze into his eyes.

"Since you ask, Miss. Wallingsford, I will say I am just making an observation. Would it bother you if I was hoping to catch your attention?"

Her heart was pounding in her ear making it hard to concentrate. Thoughts in her head were obscured like staring into the sun. Struggling to regain her head, she caught a passing logic. "Wouldn't you be happier with a woman who is from your homeland? I'm sure there are habits and traditions that I know nothing of, but which are important to you."

His smile turned softer and his blue eyes locked on hers, "Sweet woman, I only seek one who would love me as I love her. All the rest is what makes life interesting."

He stretched out 'as I love her' and she felt the heat grow the pit of her belly. Her words she'd spoke to her grandmother echoed his. Her mother had tried to set her up with a man who could take care of her and she felt bad about that. She never wanted to take advantage of a man. As a tenant farmer with nothing but a dream, that certainly wasn't the issue with him.

He was different than any man she had ever met. There had been men that openly flirted with her and she would rebuff them for their forwardness. Their obvious assertiveness seemed to be an attempt to win a challenge. Evan, however, gave her the feeling he was entirely genuine. Perhaps it was his patient control over himself. It was as though he knew she would fall in love with him and he merely needed to wait. A knowledge that was not conceited, just sure. As though he already knew the future and he was waiting for her to catch up to him. How perplexing it was for her to get her head around that thought. She was the one from the future, yet she felt like he was the one who knew what would happen.

Before she could respond he stood, took her hand and kissed it. "Now, Miss Wallingford, you must excuse me, the cords of wood won't chop themselves."

"Uh, yes. Of course." She stumbled over her words.

With a devilish grin, he said, "I will look forward to the conversation at supper." He turned and left the kitchen in two steps and a bang as the screen door slapped the door frame.

She sprung from her chair and smoothed her skirt down several times. It was unnerving how affected she was by him. She didn't want to feel these feelings. She was still licking her wounds from Andrew. She didn't know how a 19th century Scottish immigrant would respond in a relationship. What if this was all an ego-stroking play to him. She was not going to be the fool again. Maybe men from this time just jumped at any girl that would agree to cook his dinner and have his babies. What if her mother had been right? Maybe she should just worry about finding security first and love later. Her mind was racing in circles.

"Lily?" she heard Bettie calling with a strained voice.

"Bettie? Bettie, are you alright?"

Bettie bustled around the corner, "There you are! I've been calling for you. Are you alright?"

"Oh! Yes, sorry! I was just deep in thought and didn't hear you."

"Oh, good. Poor dear. You must be worried about your people. I understand." Bettie took her by the hand, "Darlin, come upstairs and I'll show you your room."

She followed Bettie up the stairs and tried to reel her thoughts into order. They walked the length of the hallway and turned into the last door on the back side of the house. A chill tingled her arms under her sleeves. The room was cool as though it had been closed up for months.

"This is an extra room we keep for guests. It hasn't been used in a while so it will take a few hours to warm."

Lily noticed a small glow of fire in the fireplace. Despite the room being closed up for a while, Lily didn't see any dust. She wondered if Bettie had just cleaned the room from top to bottom and decided the woman must be lightning fast.

"It's lovely. Are you sure you don't mind me staying here?"

"Oh, no, darlin'. You're family. This is your home too. I'm certain you would draw me in to your home if ever I was to come to your neck of the woods."

Lily tried to imagine Bettie in 2018. "Of course! I couldn't imagine anything else."

"Well, then. It's all good. You make yourself at home. We have an outhouse but in the winter months, we use a chamber pot under the bed. I'm sorry, but I don't have servants. We just haven't been able to afford them. If you would just dump it in the outhouse after breakfast in the mornings, then you don't have to go outside during the night to do your business."

"Oh sure! I can do that."

"When I get up I put on a pot of water to boil and I'll bring you a pitcher of wash water."

"Thank you. What can I do to help you?"

"I appreciate that, honeycakes. You can help me when I need it. Now, I need to tend to the wash. I'll let you have a minute to get your bearings." Bettie closed the door behind her as she left.

Lily wrapped her arms around herself. It felt safe to be tucked into a bedroom where she belonged despite not belonging in this time at all. She was an intruder. An alien. She had no idea how it really happened and even worse, she had no idea how to get home. The comfort she felt of being taken in by her ancestors covered the deep knowledge that she was a fraud. She couldn't reciprocate Bettie's offer if her life depended on it. Her home in Frankfort wasn't even built yet.

She crossed to the windows. Dark green wool curtains framed the south-facing window where the light shown through and made a quartered square that stretched across a woven grass rug on the floor. Small bubbles of air were trapped in the glass panes. As her focus shifted to the landscape behind the house, her breath caught as a zing of pleasure scorched her abdomen. Evan was swinging the ax above his head. His body strained to control the movement and she could make out the tense muscles of his thighs under the cloth of his breeches. His determined look gave her a zeal of delight as she imagined him focusing on loving her with such tenacity. Despite the cool weather, a film of perspiration glistened on his brow.

Who was this man, she wondered. Could she let herself be caught up in her feelings of attraction for a man old enough to be her grandfather's grandfather? Of course, she thought, he sure doesn't look like anyone's grandfather right now. But, she wondered, what would a life with him be like? Is he just looking for someone to have his babies and keep his house? After all, being born in the 20th century makes her a different kind of woman than he could imagine.

Her thoughts drifted into disjointed feelings and her eyes focused on the landscape before her again. The barren trees formed a protective barrier around a small field for a garden and beyond that forests and fields spread as far as the horizon. The dull brown December landscape echoed her feelings exactly. Dense thickets and spent fields mirrored her heart.

She realized the sounds had changed. The cracking of splitting wood was replaced by a serene whistle of a breeze through the gaps in the window. The sensation of someone watching her made the hairs on her scalp tingle. He was standing with his feet spread in a casual stance, his hands clasped over the handle of the ax, and a pleased grin had spread across his face. When he had her attention, he bowed and rose, and blew her a kiss.

Her first thought was shock and she nearly bolted from the window, but catching herself with a hand on the curtain, she laughed. His comfortable charm enveloped her. She shook her head, smiling, and waved him away as she turned. She couldn't help but find him incredibly intoxicating.

Chapter 4 – One-Room Schoolhouse

William Black strode through the front door, closing it with his left hand without looking back. His dark brown eyes were searching. Jet black hair lay in tamed curly locks across the crown of his head held in place with shiny pomade. As he passed through the foyer, the light of the oil wall sconce reflected in the tumbled waves. A strong jawline that ended with long black sideburns, lanky arms and legs, and his tall, strong physique all gave him a subtle imposing presence. He wore a practical brown wool suit with a white shirt showing at the neck and cuffs and brown boots that had a softened look of age but impeccable polish.

"Bettie?" he called out gently as crossed the room. He craned his neck looking around He was a contradiction of gentleness and persistence.

"Darlin!" her melodic voice sang out from the kitchen just before the swishing of her skirts could be heard. William's head riveted to the sound and the two of them nearly collided in the hallway between the rooms. Lights danced in his eyes as the smile spread across his face. His arm laced under her arm and around her tiny waist pulling her into him as it went. She let him gather her in and melted into his side.

"Sweet man," her tiny fingers caressed his ear, "I'm so glad you're home."

He bent his head down to her and tenderly kissed her mouth. Then said, "My love, you are my home."

He hugged her to his chest and inhaled the sweet scent of her rose water perfume.

Pulling back to share the news, she said, "Darlin, did you get the message that our cousin is here and she is a teacher?"

"Yes, I did. I'm anxious to become acquainted. Where is she?"

They walked into the parlor arm and arm. "Here she is! I would like you to meet our cousin Lily Wallingsford of Frankfort." Turning to Lily, "Lily, this is my dear husband, William Black."

Lily had been looking at a dried star fish with a magnifying glass when they came in. She set them down and held her breath as she turned. It wasn't every day you meet your grandfather four generations back. She had heard stories about the two of them. They were a legend. Now, staring at the two of them standing before her with their arms around each other, she was not disappointed. William stood over six feet tall, towering above Bettie. Of course, she'd always heard of her as Sarah Elizabeth but in the years between, the nick-name had gotten lost. An unmistakable aura surrounded them and permeated into the room. Love defined them.

He released Bettie and stepped forward to Lily, reaching for her hand. She let him take it. She expected a shock wave of electricity when he first touched her, but she only felt the warmth of his calloused strong hand.

"My cousin, it's a pleasure. Welcome to our home."

By some compulsion ingrained into her, she curtsied and bobbed her head, saying, "Thank you."

"Please have a seat," he gestured to a red velvet sofa. "I don't believe I have had the pleasure of meeting you. I do apologize."

"Oh no! Please don't apologize. We keep to ourselves."

"So what business brings you to Stephensport? Is your father with you?"

"Uh, no. I traveled with another woman but she went on to Owensboro. I don't seem to recall what happened next, but I ended up in the creek. Mr. McEwen found me. All we can assume is the carriage was robbed and they fled with it and my things."

"I see." He stared at her as though sizing up the story. Lily held her breath. "I will send word to your parents first thing in the morning. They will want to know, of course."

Panic seized her. She could give him the real names of her parents and then maybe the telegram would just get lost. But, what if it didn't? What if word came back that no one by that name existed? It would make them suspicious. She would have to send the letter. Only then could she have control over her story.

"Oh, let me. I would like to send it. I'll let them know how kind you have been to let me stay."

William looked concerned. It occurred to her the responsibility he would feel for her. As a woman, she had to constantly be looked after by a male relative. She tried not to roll her eyes at her own revelation.

"I'm not sure. I would feel better sending it myself. If I were your father, I would feel better hearing from the man of the house."

"I'm sure you're right, sir. However, I know this will scare them, so, perhaps a message in my own words would allay their fears."

He considered her suggestion before answering, "I understand your sentiment, however, I cannot shirk my responsibility. If you would like to include a note, that would be fine, but I will be sending out a letter first thing tomorrow."

Lily tried not to show the panic she felt. There was no way around him. Apparently, men in this time were not so easily persuaded.

"Bettie said you might be available to teach at our school until we find a new teacher, but I'm sure you will want to get back to your family, won't you?"

"Oh. Well. I came here to spend some time getting to know you all. If you don't mind me around for a while, I would be happy to fill in at your school."

"I see. Of course we would welcome time to get acquainted. I also can't deny what a help it would be to have a qualified teacher. The last three we had were useless ninnies."

"What made them useless?" She was fishing to see what not to do.

"They were young. Barely children themselves. They could not handle the boys. Therefore, there was no order. No discipline."

"I see."

"How long have you been teaching?"

"Fourt—I mean four years," she corrected.

"What would you say is your strongest talent in teaching?"

She thought a moment. It had been a long time since she had been through an interview. "Differentiating instruction to the individual needs of each student." She said it with confidence, certain that this was the most important quality in a teacher. At least a teacher in 2018. She wasn't at all sure what a teacher in 1889 would be prized for.

He sat in the occasional chair closest to Bettie who was listening intently. He pinched the ends of his handle bar mustache. "Did you say 'different aiding'?"

She realized he didn't know what the word was. It was probably a new concept made up in her time. "It's like that, 'different aiding'. It's where you teach to each child's needs rather than teaching one lesson for all kids."

"How *else* would you teach students in multiple grades?"

Her mind locked up. She had always complained to other teachers that she had at least seven different levels of reading ability in her 4th grade class. At least they were all about ten years old. She tried to wrap her head around the idea of having a class that ranged in age from six to fourteen. A first grader sitting with a high school freshman. Yes, that would be differentiating.

"Right, well, that tells you I can do it." She tried to sound confident.

"You have a point there. The last girl gave one lesson and the little ones cried and the older ones got bored and ran roughshod over her." He paused to gauge her reaction. He must have determined she was worth a shot because he then told her, "Then if you are sure, let's have you start tomorrow. Understand you will have to be a substitute until the town council can meet and agree. They may stop by the school to observe your methods."

"That will be fine. What time does school begin?"

"Eight o'clock."
***

The next morning Lily stood next to Mr. Black in the front of the classroom. She scanned the faces of the young pupils. It was mid-year and the fresh excitement of returning to school was long gone. They looked at her from head to toe as though sizing her up.

"Students," Mr. Black began, "I would like to introduce Miss Wallingsford. She will be your teacher for a while as we continue to look for a permanent teacher. Please give her your best behavior."

With a short bow to her, he turned and practically darted from the classroom.

Some people just aren't comfortable in a classroom, she thought. She took a deep breath to calm her nerves and set the tone. She knew the best way to begin with a new group of students was to practice classroom behavior drills and team building exercises.

With her smoothest teacher voice and a big smile, she started, "Good morning, class. I'm so glad to be your teacher. I know we are going to have a great time learning—"

She stopped mid-sentence when the door opened and a tall, lanky young man stepped into the classroom. She sucked in a breath as her eyes opened wide. She wondered if he had seen her come into the school and followed her. Surely he was not planning to try to assault her in front of the children.

Gaining her strength, "Excuse me! What are you doing here?"

He stopped when he saw her and an oily grin spread across his face. "Well I was coming t' school," he said with a snarky tone, "but I'd come sooner if I'd known we had a saucy new teacher." He slid into a seat without taking his eyes off her.

Her heart was pounding. She gripped the edge of her desk behind her trying to collect her thoughts. Not twenty-four hours earlier, this boy tried to assault her. She forced herself to look away and her eyes landed on a tiny little girl in the front row. Her long brown braids lay over the shoulders of her dark blue dress. The girl's blue eyes watched her with such an innocent gaze. Lily wondered how different this girl was than little girls her age in 2018. She knew that little girls she taught looked at her as though she were a super hero.

That was all Lily needed. The faith of this little girl welled up in her. She determined that the tall boy needed her as much as the little girl. She just had to figure out how to reach him.

"Students, let's go over a few rules to make it easier for everyone to have fun learning." A stillness crept through the room. She noticed a few students looking at her confused. "Surely you have had rules in this school. Why the confused looks?"

A hand shot up in the second row. A boy that looked to be about nine or ten squirmed in his seat before asking, "Ma'am, what does fun have to do with school?"

Her heart sank. "For a few days until I learn your names, please tell me your name when you are called on. What is your name?"

"I'm Thomas, ma'am."

"Thank you. Help me understand what your routine has been so far this year, Thomas."

"We sing hymns. Then we memorize scripture verses and come to you to be checked. Then we have lunch for an hour. Then we learn geography. Then the girls learn sewing or go home early while the boys practice writing and arithmetic. Then we go home at 3:00."

Lily's mind was reeling. "So you use the bible as your reading book? That's how you learn to read?"

Thomas nodded.

"And the girls don't learn to write or do math?"

"You mean arithmetic? No. They don't need to."

Lily glanced from one girl's face to the next. Most were expressionless, but she noticed at least two that pursed their lips in displeasure of this system.

"You, you in the pink dress." She had noticed her frown at the boy's explanation. "Do you want to learn arithmetic?"

"My name is Faith, ma'am. Yes. I want to learn arithmetic. I know I can understand it if someone taught me."

"Yes. I agree, Faith." She looked at them all trying to figure out how to proceed. "You, young man in the back," she looked at the tall boy. "What do you want to learn about?"

He smirked and stared at her briefly, then said, "I don't *want* to learn nothing. I only come here because my pop will beat me senseless if I cut school."

"Well, what do you plan to do when you get done with school? How old are you?"

He swelled up as big as his chest would go, "I'm fourteen. I'm getting as far from this town as possible, as soon as I can. I got a job lined up on a steamboat."

"I see. That sounds exciting."

"Yeah. Well, a monkey's elbow would probably excite you, too, then."

Laughter broke out among the older boys who also watched to see how she would handle the disrespect.

"What did you say your name was," she paused before adding, "sir?"

He stopped laughing with his buddies and turned. He looked down his nose at her but with parted lips of surprise. She knew he expected her to blast him. She had purposely tried to reach him in a different way. If he wanted to get far away from this town, it was possibly likely because he wasn't getting any respect as a person in some part of his life. He didn't feel valued.

"Uh, my name is Joseph," pausing, "ma'am."

She smiled at him in thanks for the respect reciprocated. "Joseph, I don't know what job you have lined up on the steamboat, but if you knew how to read maps, factor speed and distance formulas, and calculate coal consumption, do you think you would have a better chance being successful in that career?"

She saw a glimmer of hope in him as the light danced in his dark brown eyes, but just as quickly some negative thought over-rode the new path. "I ain't got time to learn all that stuff." He turned away to end the conversation.

She turned around to hide the smile that spread on her face. There was a dreamer still in there and it wouldn't take much to find him. She wrote her name on the corner of the board and then told them about herself, sticking to hobbies and experiences they wouldn't think was crazy.

Then she continued, "So, now you know a bit about me the person. Now I will tell you about me the teacher." They all looked at her waiting. "You have probably never met a teacher like me. I learned to be a teacher at a place very far from here. First of all, I think learning should be fun. I want you to enjoy it. If you enjoy learning now, you will seek to learn all your life. Secondly, I believe you can all learn anything you want to, no matter if you are a boy or girl." She paused waiting for their reaction. Several of the girls' mouths gaped open.

"Yes! You can. If you want to learn it. It may take some students longer than others, but that's fine. Lastly, we have to feel safe here," she glanced at Joseph, "and respect each other. So we have to have some predictable routines. Let's practice walking into school and going to our seats without talking or being disruptive."

Over the course of the morning, she found that they were exceedingly well-trained in the rituals of school life. What surprised her, though, was their lack of creative thought and their great ability to stay engaged in an activity for long periods of time. They had incredible stamina for persevering through an assignment, but only when she had given them the ground work of exactly what to do. They were trained soldiers never questioning her methods, at least not out loud.

As the last student filed out at two o'clock, she realized she felt exhausted. Being present in the moment for hours on end takes a toll and she felt it. Though she was in her element in a classroom, she was a fish out of water here. The norms of her classroom back home couldn't be further from reality. The one thing she had expected and found to be true was that children are children no matter where or when. They need someone who cares about them and believes in them. In order to feel safe, they needed someone who knows what to do.

She closed the door and walked back to her desk to plan for tomorrow. A whistling wind blew through the cracks around the door. She sat down in front of the stack of slates. She chuckled to herself. She wasn't going to be able to lug home totes full of slates. The whistling stopped briefly and she looked up in time to see a man closing the door behind him.

She recognized him as the man at the Fine Clothes Mercantile. Conflicted emotions of lust and anger made it hard to think. His snobbery clouded her impression of him. Despite the riveting feeling she got when his eyes locked on hers, she couldn't bear how he'd looked down on Evan.

"Can I help you, sir?" she asked curtly.

"Yes, Miss Wallingsford? Am I correct?"

"Yes. That's me."

A curl of a smile turned up on one side of his mouth. "Good. I was looking for you."

"Me? Whatever for?"

He sat on the corner of her desk and looked down at her. Determined not to be looked down on, she stood up and crossed her arms. He smirked again recognizing her behavior as defiance of his authority.

"Yes, Miss Wallingsford. Perhaps Mr. Black failed to mention my position on the town council. Not surprising. He must have a great deal on his mind with the farm work and all."

It would have been a considerate thing to say except that she could hear the condescending tone. He didn't have menial things to worry about like farm work. He apparently considered farmers to be a lower class.

He continued, "Not to worry. I just came by to introduce myself and ask you a few questions. Just to get to know our new teacher better." He walked around behind her and leaned in as he passed. He breathed deeply and closed his eyes with obvious pleasure. Lily couldn't see the conflict inside him as he looked like his mouth watered for a piece of warm cake. Regaining his composure, he squinted his eyes and pinched the bridge of his nose. "I take personal responsibility for the academic achievement of our young people."

"I see. I must say I'm a bit surprised. You don't look like someone with such a social conscience." *More like he is concerned with his social calendar*, she thought.

He shifted his weight and leaned toward her on one hand. His eyes were magnetic. She couldn't look away. He was close enough that the scent of sandlewood tickled her

71

nose. It was a clean, neat scent, but strong. She stopped herself from closing her eyes to get lost in it. She would not be pulled into his charisma. His eyes slowly took inventory of her face and hair and then drifted down to her bosom. He was flagrantly sizing her up. Being in a different class, he must feel he has the privilege of treating people any way he chooses. She was about to tell him to just get out when he said the one thing she couldn't ignore.

"Miss Wallingford, you are an exceedingly beautiful woman who no doubt must have a man panting after your hand."

All the while, his gaze never wavered. She felt hypnotized. Where all men in this time so forthright. She would have thought it was the biggest come on she had ever heard, but he stood up, walked in front of her, and took her left hand in his and kissed it.

"*What was he trying to do? Was this his way of asking a girl out? Was he just bowled over by her appearance?*" she thought. She really had no idea what the rules were of different classes at this time.

"Mr.—Um, Mr. What did you say your name is?" She felt a bit lightheaded. "*Am I swooning? Maybe this is normal for rubbing elbows with the upper class.*"

Immediate heat radiated from her face. She was so embarrassed at herself for letting this guy get to her. She bit her lip, mad at herself. Now he will see me blush and think I'm a ditzy school girl!

He lowered her hand but still held it, "Everbright. Brian Everbright. Perhaps you saw my family's mercantile on Main Street?"

"*Who was he kidding? There was a connection between the glances and she knew it!*"

"Oh, yes." She regained her composure as she remembered the day before. "Mr. Everbright," she pulled her hand out of his, "did you want to discuss curriculum? Perhaps plan a PLC meeting?"She felt snarky now.

She hoped the effect of her words would be a cold pan of water as she rebuffed his attention. However, it seemed to just stoke his fire. He slowly walked behind her as he continued to take note of every curve the tight bodice revealed. She turned to face him.

"Well?" she asked.

"Truly, of course, my dear. I'm not familiar with a PLC, though."

"A professional learning community? No? Maybe there is one area where I am the expert." Anger was getting the better of her now.

He didn't waver. Lily could see the depth of his upbringing in his lack of response to her goading. "I expect the boys to be able to recite the Bible with chapter and verse. They should have a good understanding of arithmetic. They need to be able to write using proper grammar and sentence structure by age fourteen. Have excellent penmanship. Whenever I walk into the school, I expect to find order and industrious endeavor."

The blood drained from her face as she stood there with her mouth open. "And what about the girls?"

He waved off-handedly, "Of course, of course. They need to be able to read the Bible and recite it so they will learn to be chaste God-fearing women."

"That's it?"

"Certainly. What else would the boys learn? I suppose if you want to throw in a good dose of geography, I can see how it would be useful."

"I mean for the girls."

He shook his head confused. "They don't need to know anything else. Filling their head with lofty ideas will only make them discontent at home. You wouldn't want to ruin them, would you? No man would have them."

"No man would have them? Is that their purpose?"

He laughed at her absurdity. "My dear, as a woman, a women who has apparently been overly choosy which is certainly to be commended, you surely must know the desperate station of old maids. Especially old maids who lack resources. Besides being a burden on their family, they are sentenced to a life of poverty. We cannot hope that for our female students."

She was dumbfounded. Did he actually just insinuate that she was old or was that a compliment? Or both? Maybe she hadn't thought this through. She certainly didn't want to subject the girls to less opportunity. What did she know of the pitfalls of being a woman in the 1800s?

Reason flooded back to her. "Wait! That is not giving these girls credit. If they had the same opportunities as men, they would be just as successful at whatever endeavor they attempted. I can't speak for men marrying them, but they surely would be able to support themselves. Besides, if men are afraid of what women can do with a level playing field, that doesn't say much for men."

He closed his eyes before speaking, "Miss Wallingsford, you are a charming young woman. I daresay you have a keen mind. Therefore, I would suggest you put it to use in ways that will benefit your students and yourself."

"And I suppose you know what those ways are?"

"Yes. Yes, I do. I would be happy to guide you in the right direction. We will start by teaching a curriculum as I have laid out. Then, I will help you understand the benefits of being an attractive young woman." He winked at her.

She wanted to slap him but sucked in a sharp breath before speaking instead. "And just how would you go about helping me understand that?" She tried not to sound sarcastic.

He stepped closer and caressed her cheek with his finger. His eyes admired the milky white skin of her face and neck. "A beautiful woman is a gift from God to be adored. Would you let me adore you?" Now he looked into her eyes with all seriousness. He'd broke character. She could see a wild desire now where solemn aloofness had prevailed. He was most certainly torn between staying in his own world and wanting her. She swallowed hard. Her Prince Charming was back and obviously had a crush on her.

Shocked at his answer, shocked at her guttural response, she couldn't manage to speak at all. Instead she found herself leaning into his hand and nudging him to touch her more.

He whispered, "I'll take that as a yes." He reached down and took her hand and kissed it again. "Now, I must go." He looked at her with a pained look. "I do wonder if it's possible. You have an effect on me that is undeniable. You will hear from me soon."

In a swirl of his coat, the air rushed over her and brought her back to her senses. Thoughts tumbled in her head like jagged saws bumping and falling to the ground. Part of her longed for more of his touch, more of his intoxicating attention. The rest of her recoiled from his patronizing authoritarianism. She'd be damned if she was not going to teach the girls everything she taught the boys. The door clicked as he closed it with controlled force behind him.

She leaned back on the desk, exhausted and overwhelmed. She could still feel the caress of his finger on her cheek and down the side of her neck. She closed her eyes and ran her hand across her face. She let herself imagine Brian taking that caress a step further, pulling her against him with an arm around her waist, warm, soft lips covering hers. She could smell the sandalwood soap. His warm breath with a hint of the mint leaf he was chewing buffeted her cheek. Her body molded to his as he pulled her even closer.

"Are ye done in, Miss Wallingsford? Perhaps you should sit down. You look like you might pass out."

She jolted back to reality and focused on Evan's face. His sapphire blue eyes leveled on her with gentle propriety. She could see it in his look: he offered her the key to his heart and all she had to do was claim it.

"Mr. McEwen, you startled me." She stuffed down her emotions that had run rampant in her daydream.

"Did I now?" He gave her a sideways glance.

"What do you need?"

"I dinna need anything. I just came to check on ye and see how your first day went."

She relaxed, loosening her shoulders. "Oh. How kind. It went very well. They are a very well-behaved group of students."

A chuckle erupted from his throat, "That's not what the last teacher thought!"

"Really?" She was surprised. Despite the wholly different ideology of teaching they had been used to, they were very quiet. Not like her students back home that were chatter boxes with way too much energy. In fact, now that she thought about it, she didn't have to stop for a 'brain break' or to 'get the wiggles out' once.

In 2018, she would have to stop for a two or three minute break where the students would dance or exercise to a video to let off excess energy. Especially after long periods of intense school work, they would become so restless they could no longer pay attention.

"Maybe she just wasn't as a good a teacher as you," he offered.

She pursed her lips, "They probably are just trying to figure out my weaknesses first."

"Hm. Are you ready to go home? I'll walk with you."

She thought about the pile of slates on the desk. "I really need to finish grading these so I can get them back to the students tomorrow."

"That's fine. I need to stop by the blacksmith. I'll come by for you on my way back, then."

"Thank you."

He left and she finished the grading. It was a simple assignment. They just had to write their name and tell one thing about themselves. She wanted to gauge how well they could write letters. As she suspected. The girls could barely write. The younger boys could print neatly and the older boys had perfect cursive. Brian's curriculum requirements bore out the teaching of the previous teachers.

How could a girl get through eighth grade and not be able to sign her name? She supposed it was possible in a world where women had no need to ever sign their name. It was all completely foreign to her. She tried to imagine being a woman in that time and having no say, no legal right to own anything whether it was a bank account or land. Everything a woman had would have to be run through a man. A male relative. A person who could disagree with her wishes and do as they pleased with their assets. The woman would have no say in it. Even if he squandered it away on gambling, she would have no rights.

She shook her head. In such circumstances, whom you marry would make a remarkable difference. The man you allow yourself to be tied to would have all authority over every part of your life. In her time, women considered looks, money, chemistry and love, with love usually having the greatest weight. In this time, a man's temperament would be critical, right before having the means to take care of her. Without the ability to work, a woman would depend solely on his wealth for security. Love, looks, and chemistry were perks in the deal.

And how, she thought, did men of this time size up women? It appeared that it depended on the class of the man. A working-class man would need a woman that could shoulder the domestic work well. A socialite man would need a well-bred civilized woman preferably with a dowry that would increase his wealth and net worth. Looks were favorable, but not necessary. Intelligence was not only not necessary, it could be a hindrance to a man if she tried to assert herself and get in his way. A perfect woman in 1889 would be a beautiful ignorant woman that kept her opinions to herself and was capable of running a genteel civilized household complete with well-attended parties.

She sighed with grief. What a mess she was in. She knew she could turn heads and she was maybe capable of running a genteel household. She was also highly educated and quite opinionated. Brian's words, *'you wouldn't want to ruin them'* came to mind.

Evan returned and they locked up the school and left. She hadn't figured out what she was going to do. She had a basic lesson prepared for school the next day. As Brian instructed, she had the boys and girls lessons divided. It galled her. She had been trained to teach to all students, no matter their ability. Students with less ability were to be given special instruction to bring them up to speed and students who were

advanced were to be given more challenging work to develop them further.

"Ye seem very quiet, Miss. Wallingsford." Evan said.

She was pulled out of her intense internal argument. "I'm just trying to figure out how to please the town council without compromising what I know is best."

"Hm," he thought about what she said. "What're they wanting ye to do that has ye riled?"

She wasn't sure she wanted to tell him. Maybe he would feel the same way as Brian. After all, he was looking for a woman who would unquestioningly take care of his home and have babies. She decided to test the waters.

"I wanted to teach the girls to write." This seemed innocuous enough.

"That seems reasonable. In my country, boys and girls are required to attend school until they are thirteen. There are girls' schools if a family wants to send their daughter there instead of the free school. But, all students learn the same content."

She breathed a sigh of relief. "Why do you think the town council doesn't want me to teach the girls here to write?"

"It seems a bit backwards."

"Mr. Everbright said I would ruin them."

He jerked around, "Ruin them? What an idiot."

"So you wouldn't mind if your wife could write and had educated opinions?"

"Not at all. How could I have a conversation with my wife if I had to explain ever'thing? Likely Mr. Everbright wants someone he can push around and won't argue with him."

"And Scottish women argue with their husbands?"

He laughed out loud, "They'd argue if they were educated or not. At least if they're educated, they make sense!"

She laughed.

"Nay. I've had many a heated conversation with my sisters and often as not, they were right."

"So you think I should teach the girls to write?"

"I can't answer that for ye. I think ye already know what yer going to do though."

She smiled looking down at the ground. Evan certainly seemed used to women who had their own opinions. He wasn't afraid of that, from what she could tell.

They reached a secluded stretch of path between thick leafless bushes sleeping the winter away. Without warning, he took her hand and pulled her to him.

"Miss Wallingsford, the passion ye have for yer students tells me there's a fire in you. It excites me greatly. Ye remind me of the women at home that would fiercely protect their family."

The depth of his longing was evident in his eyes. She wasn't sure what he wanted her to say next. All propriety in her mind screamed for her to protest his forthrightness, but she couldn't. She didn't want to move. She wanted to stay in his hot embrace and feel the adoration he had for her.

He must have taken her lack of protest as consent because he pulled her even closer and kissed her. The scent of cedar filled her senses. She wasn't sure if it was from him or some magic that had catapulted her into his time and arms. The sharp woodsy scent and the rush of emotion inside her seized her breath until she nearly fainted.

He gently released her, holding her steady as she regained composure. Looping her hand onto his arm, they strolled forward silently in their thoughts.

They reached the porch and went in the house. Bettie was bustling about dusting the parlor. The aroma of chicken, sage, and rosemary filled Lily's nose. She hummed an 'mmm' out loud.

"Welcome home, you two. How did your first day go, Lily?"

"Oh, fine. They're good kids. I think we will be fine together."

Bettie gave Evan a sideways glance.

"What was that look for?" Lily asked.

"We just haven't had good luck with teachers staying long. There must be something about that group of kids. That's all."

"I see." She sat down on the velvet sofa. "They behaved perfectly. I am used to a whole lot worse than that."

"Things must be bad in Frankfort, I imagine, then," said Bettie.

Bettie and Evan took seats in the two occasional chairs in front of the sofa.

"Oh my, I almost forgot," said Bettie and she jumped back up and went to the fireplace mantle. "This came for you today." She handed Lily a parchment envelope.

The envelope was small and stiff. It reminded her of the fancy paper you would buy to print off your resume'. The name 'Miss Wallingsford' was written in a flourish in black ink. She had seen fonts for wedding invitations that weren't that elaborate.

She turned it over. It was sealed with wax with a big E in the middle. She pulled the flap open and pulled out the notepaper folded in half. She didn't see Evan make a face at Bettie.

Dear Miss Wallingsford, the pleasure of your company is requested for supper on the morrow. I'll send my carriage for you. Best regards, Brian Everbright.

She looked up at them. They were waiting patiently.

"Well. What did it say?" Bettie let out.

"Brian Everbright has invited me to dinner. Tomorrow."

Evan didn't say anything, but his face turned a shade of red.

"I don't even know where he lives," she said.

Now he exploded. "Ye aren't actually going to go are ye?"

"I, well, I guess so. I mean, I don't want to be rude."

He made a snorting noise and then looked at the ceiling.

"Apparently, you don't approve." Lily said.

Bettie piped in, "Now, Mr. McEwen, you can have your opinions. However, getting an invitation from a man like Mr. Everbright is a feather in a young lady's bonnet. She must decide for herself."

"Wait a minute! It's just an invitation to dinner. Not a marriage proposal. Cool down, Mr. McEwen. I'm sure he just wants to talk about the school," said Lily.

"I just think it's a bad idea. Brian Everbright doesn't do anything that doesn't somehow improve his lot or entertain him. He's a revolving door of ladies he uses and drops. And those ladies are all upper crust. What designs do you think he has on you?"

"Are you insinuating I am going to let him use me?" she said aghast.

"I just think he is not in yer best interest. Do what ye want. It's not up to me." He stormed out of the room with his eyes on her like lasers.

Bettie and Lily looked at each other. Lily smirked.

"You can't blame him," Bettie said. "It's obvious he has designs on you."

"Designs?" Lily's eyebrows shot up. "As in planned out our future? Don't you think that is jumping the gun?"

"Of course not, dear. He's a healthy young man. You're beautiful. And, you're right under his nose. He practically saved you from succumbing to shock beside the creek."

Lily turned her head toward the window. A gentle breeze blew the bare limbs of the maple tree in the yard. She couldn't deny that Evan did something to her. He had a raw, rugged appeal. She wondered what it would be like to be held in his strong arms. He seemed like a good man. Hardworking and loyal. He was a man that could love her very soul. Even so, being the wife of a man like him would be hard. Everything he would ever have would come from the sweat of his brow, and hers. He was also a man that would mean it when he said he would love her always. Wasn't that what she always wanted? Why didn't that seem like enough now?

Brian Everbright, assuming his invitation was of a personal interest, would keep her well-cared for. She would want for nothing. Her mother would have been thrilled. That cinched it for her. She would go see what Mr. Everbright had to say.

Her materialistic internal argument was settled, but something nudged the back of her mind. Images of Stephensport in 2018 formed in her mind. It was a sleepy riverside hamlet of a handful of homes. No stores. No hotels. No steamboats or passenger trains. Forgotten by time except for a few farmers and humble country folk. What happened to the Brian Everbrights of this time? Clearly, the likes of Evan McEwen were the only ones that could promise forever.

Evan didn't have supper with them that evening at the house. Lily was not surprised. She snuggled into her covers as she shivered against a chill in the winter air. The cotton pillow case felt cool against her cheek. She closed her eyes and fatigue made her dizzy. She let herself fall deeper into the topsy-turvy world of darkness. Images of the school kids flitted through her mind. Slates and chalk. Brian Everbright and his perfectly combed and oiled hair appeared before her eyes. His gray-blue haunting eyes looked at from the other side of his long nose. He leaned in and his soft lips brushed against hers. His breath smelled of mint. She breathed in the scent of him. Then Evan's face took his place. Cerulean blue pools of ocean locked her in a hold. His arms wrapped around her and pulled her into him. She felt the heat of his skin beneath the coarse cotton tunic. Her hands inched up his arms and the muscles tightened. His arms were rock hard and too big for her to get her hand around. Her breath quickened as he pressed his lips into her neck. She let out an audible sigh of ecstasy and her eyes flew open.

She looked around to make sure she was alone. Her heart pounded in her chest. The darkness hid her, but she felt like she was being watched. She wondered if it was merely because she was an outsider here or was she truly being watched? Letting out a huff, her head fell back on the pillow and she stared at the white ceiling, now a pale gray by ambient moonlight. A sound reached her ears like a trombone or a baritone. A low moan. The tone sharpened to a far-away ringing. It seemed familiar but she didn't know why. Her heart pounded and she looked toward the window. In a matter of seconds, the tone diminished and was gone. She felt totally alone again. She pulled the cover closer and drifted into a fitful sleep.

PART II

Chapter 5 – An Invitation

Priscilla Ames sat at her desk watching every move Lily made. Her dark eyelashes batted her cheeks when she blinked. Her brown cotton dress was clean but had seen better days. The seam across the shoulder that attached the sleeve had a zigzag that made Lily wonder if it had been mended from a mishap. A new pale pink ribbon looped around the neck and lay in a neat bow under Priscilla's chin. It was a desperate attempt to freshen the hand-me-down dress.

"Priscilla, could you read to me the twenty-third Psalm?" Lily asked.

"Yes, Miss Wallingsford," she beamed with wide eyes.

As the girl began to read, Lily realized she was reciting from memory despite giving the appearance of following a text with her finger. Priscilla was twelve. Lily could tell she was bright by the way she watched the others in class. She would mouth the answers silently to herself when others were called on. When Priscilla finished, Lily decided she needed to talk to her privately.

"Class, I would like each of you to read that passage silently to yourself until you are sure you can read each word. Then move on to the twenty-forth psalm."

She waited a minute for them to start working, then whispered to Priscilla, "Priscilla, would you come to my desk?"

"Yes, ma'am." Priscilla got up and tiptoed to the front.

"Priscilla, I want you to know how pleased I am with how much you understand."

Priscilla's eyes lit up with delight and her cheeks reddened.

"Have you ever thought about what you might like to do when you grow up?"

The girl's face froze in confusion. "Uh, no, Miss Wallingsford. I guess I will just be a wife and mother like my momma."

Lily sighed and smirked. "Yes, well. I'm sure your mother is a wonderful wife and mother. And you would be too. But, I wonder if you have ever daydreamed about doing any other kind of work."

Priscilla's forehead pressed down into her eyebrows. "Other kind of work? What do you mean? Like taking in wash or sewing?"

Lily shook her head. This was harder than she thought. "No, I mean, well, have you ever thought of being a writer or studying medicine or inventing things?"

Priscilla's eyes nearly popped out of her head, "No. No, ma'am. I'm certain I would have no idea how to do such things. Why would I ever think about things like that?"

"Because I think you are very smart. I think you are capable of it."

"But ma'am, I don't even know how to write. How could I ever be a writer?"

Lily sighed thoughtfully, "Priscilla, writing is a skill. You just have to be taught. No one is born knowing how to write."

The girl's mouth fell open as she took in the thought. "But, but ma'am, girls aren't taught to write."

"I understand, sweet girl. Girls here aren't taught. But there are girls that are taught. And they can learn to write as well as any man."

Priscilla stood there with her eyes wide again. Then her face fell and she looked down. "No, ma'am. I can't learn to write. It would take time away from my chores. I have to go straight home with the other girls to start chores. The boys stay to learn to write, but I have chores to do in the afternoon before my brothers get home."

"I see." Lily was the stumped one now. "What if I talked to your mother and father?"

"Oh, no, ma'am. Please don't. If I'm any trouble, Pa will tan my hide."

"Oh. Well, I don't want you to get in trouble. I will think of something. But tell me, Priscilla, would you like to learn to write?"

"I would, yes, but I still don't know what good it would do me. It's not like I'll go to high school or anything."

"I'm glad to hear you are open to the idea. You may take your seat now."

Lily decided then and there it was time to introduce the girls to a little career exploration. They had been raised to think their only option was to marry and raise a family. She couldn't imagine what that must be like. She had been prompted to dream of what she wanted to be when she grew up since she was able to speak.

"Class, when I tell you to begin, I would like the boys to pair up as we practiced yesterday and work together to compose a letter to the town council expressing what you would like to learn in school. You will create one letter as a pair."

The boys groaned.

"Girls, I would like you to gather around on the rug for a discussion with me. You may all move to your places to begin."

The boys picked up their tablets and chalk and the whole class then got up and moved to their assigned places. The girls moved to the rug and sat in two rows of a semi-circle around a chair. Lily sat in the chair and waited for the boys to begin to work, scanning her eyes across the room to make sure all the pairs were busy. Then she took a deep breath and looked around at the huddle of femininity.

"Young ladies," she noticed Priscilla watching her with fascinated interest, "I want to talk about some famous women in history, some even living now, who have chosen to pursue what interested them."

She waited a minute. They were all transfixed on her words. She could tell they were eager to hear what she had to say. Not one protested. She searched her mind for examples and the first to come to mind was Clara Barton.

"Have any of you heard of a woman named Clara Barton?" They shook their heads. "Clara Barton was, is, I guess, a woman that followed the Union troops during the Civil War. She provided aid to the soldiers. Later after the war, she would go to places that were affected by disasters and offer relief aid. She started and runs an organization called the American Red Cross. It helps a great many people." Lily was a bit fuzzy on the dates of her life, so she hoped they didn't ask too many questions.

"What about Louis May Alcott? Anyone heard of her?" They shook their heads. "She was a writer. She wrote a book called Little Women that is wonderful literature. I'm certain its popularity will continue for at least another hundred years."

She tried to think of other women. Amelia Earhart hadn't been born yet. Same for the physicist Marie Curry that would win a Noble Prize.

"There have been women who have led political movements like Joan of Arc and, oh, Susan B. Anthony. What I'm trying to say is, I would like you to think about what really interests you. It may be that you really want to raise a family, and that's fine. But you may also wish you could heal people when they are sick or injured. Or heal animals. You may have stories in your head that you wish you could write down and share with others. You may have strong feelings about what is right and wrong in society and want to change how people think and live. Your homework assignment for tonight is to imagine if you were a man, what would you want to be when you grew up."

They all stared at her wide eyed. A girl of about fourteen raised her hand.

"Yes, dear," said Lily.

"Ma'am, my daddy will get powerful mad if he finds out you are talking to us about stuff like this."

"Why do you say that?"

"I just know, ma'am. He tells me to be quiet and let him make the decisions. He has plans for me to marry a boy he knows and he says I don't have a say in it."

"For right now, let's just keep this to ourselves. I understand what you are saying and I don't want you to get in trouble until you have a chance to think it through. But, you have a mind God gave you. No one can tell you what you should think. Do you understand that?"

Lily looked from one delicate face to another. They nodded and most of them made a secretive curl of a smile as they got up and tiptoed back to their desks.

Lily dismissed the students for the day and began reading the letters the boys had written to the town council. She was curious what they would say. The comments were all over the place. They ranged from learning to make a volcano to how to drive a steam locomotive. They wanted to know how to build a house and they wanted to know how to read the stars and predict the weather. The boys had much clearer dreams about what they wanted to master in this life. She wished the girls had been given more opportunities to dream.

***

Brian walked into the conservatory to find his mother. She was watering lilies in pots with small wood dowels driven down into the soil beside the stems. The stems were tied to the dowel rods with twine to keep them standing upright and straight despite the heavy weight of their flowers.

"Mother, I need to speak with you."

"Certainly, dear. What can I do for you?"

"It's about our guest tonight," he paused.

"The school teacher, yes. So kind of you to invite her over. We should always support the working class and show them our appreciation."

Brian stiffened and squinted. "Of course, however, I would like to discuss with you the possibility that she," he stopped. He hesitated and plunged in. "The possibility that she might be thought of as more than a teacher. It's just, you know well that I have had trouble finding a companion that doesn't," he struggled to find the words. "Someone who doesn't bore me."

His mother turned to him, "Son, a wife's job is to complement your station. Not entertain you."

He took a deep breath. "Mother, I believe this girl would make me happy. And, the business is thriving. Could you just give her a chance? I don't know much about her life in Frankfort but perhaps she has friends in Frankfort that would be of use to us."

"My dearest son, enjoy a dalliance. I will, of course, be ever gracious, as is my duty. Don't get your heart set on an impossible situation, though. This school teacher would be crushed in our society circles and you know it. There are plenty of suitable ladies that I will introduce you to in Lexington. Don' give up so easily."

***

Walking home, she remembered Mr. Everbright's invitation. His carriage would be by to get her soon. She wondered what he would want to discuss over dinner. Was this just a polite social appointment or was he truly interested in her.

She climbed the stairs to the porch and let herself in the door. She realized she had not seen Evan since their conversation where he expressed his opinion of the invitation. She missed him. She missed talking to him. She didn't have time to stay in her reverie, though. Bettie met her at the door.

"There you are, missy. Now let's get you upstairs and get you ready. I hope you don't mind. I freshened up one of my dresses for you to wear to dinner."

"What's the big deal, Bettie?"

"What's the big deal? Honey, have you got a fever? A man like him comes calling, you need to take this seriously. Not that I'm one to chase money, but you'd be a fool not to hear him out and try to look your best. Momma always said you can fall in love with a rich man just as easy as a poor one. Just my luck I fell in love with a poor one. You though, it isn't written in stone yet." She grabbed Lily by the hand and pulled her up the stairs. "And there was once a time that I ran in the same circles as Brian Everbright, though he would never believe it. I can get you ready so that you will fit right in."

Bettie sat her on the stool in front of the vanity and started pulling pins from her hair and brushing in long forceful strokes. It actually felt good to Lily. It was like a scalp massage. The soft horse hair brush made shushing noises as it traveled down the lengths of hair. Bette worked like a professional. When she had run the brush through about a hundred times, Lily's blond hair was shining like the sun. Bettie pulled it up on the sides and secured it with combs. Then she pulled two small strands out from near her temples. Letting them hang down for the moment, she pulled up the back into a twist and pinned it. Then she braided the two strands and pinned them into the twist on either side of her head. She dug in a drawer until she found two thin matching ribbons which she wove around each braid and then tied into one bow at the top of the twist.

She had Lily stand up and began to unbutton the day dress. Carefully pulling it over her head, she hung it in an armoire. Then, Bettie pulled a yellow silk dress out and gathered it up to put over Lily's head. Lily ducked under and lifted her hands to find the arm holes. The heavy silk layers fell around her like morning light streaming over a meadow. Bettie secured the hook and eyes until the dress hugged Lily like a glove. Bettie stepped back to look at how it fit.

"My word, child. This dress must have been made for you and not me. I never did it justice like you do. Of course, it hasn't fit the same since I had Carlton." She turned Lily around to look at her from all sides. "Oh, wait now." Bettie tore out of the room and was back in a flash. "Here," she had a gold watch on a chain that she lowered onto Lily's bosom and then fastened at the back of her neck. "It'll give you a little sparkle. It's the only nice jewelry I have."

Lily picked it up and looked at it more closely. It was cold to the touch and had delicate etched flowers adorning the gold locket of a pocket watch. "Oh, thank you, Bettie. I'll be careful with it."

Just about the time Bettie was helping her slip into a wool coat, there was a knock at the door. A few moments later, they heard Carlton announce that Miss Wallingsford's carriage was here. Lily looked at her reflection in the hand mirror. She barely recognized the Victorian woman looking back at her. This woman seemed so far from 2018, so frozen in time. The longer she stayed here, the more disconnected she felt to her own life.

"Are you ready, darlin'?" Bettie asked.

She put the mirror down and gave Bettie a long look. It seemed so out of character for her to entertain thoughts of Brian Everbright. She felt entirely conflicted and knew she shouldn't have agreed to see him, but a certain thrill gripped her when she thought of him. A clinching zing of electricity grabbed at her insides. Maybe this is what made him different from all the men her mother would try to set her up with. She never felt anything for them. They didn't set off any alarms. She never daydreamed about them. It just felt so forced. The absolute only attraction they had for her was the fact that they had money. She hated the fact that money was the only thing attractive about them. It made her feel dirty even when they used their money to attract her. It was a pathetic game where they both knew the truth but never spoke of it. She had to admit, his obvious wealth and social station was icing on the cake.

94

Brian Everbright intrigued her. In a deep secret part of her heart, she wanted nothing more than for him to find her as fascinating her she found him. The electricity between them was tangible. He was intrigued by her and that made her dizzy with arousal. That would be even one more way that he was different. The men she had dated didn't seem excited by her older body. They didn't care if she had an opinion or a brain either. They just seemed desperate not to be alone.

She came out of her reverie to find herself in an open carriage pulling up in front of a large stone house with white columns. They had not travelled far but the house was set back in the trees and it seemed like Stephensport was a world away. The driver hopped down and helped her out of the carriage. She smoothed down the folds of the satin apron across the front of the dress but stopped when she heard the creak of the front door opening.

Brian Everbright made long purposeful steps toward her. He wore a tuxedo with tails. His hair shined like it was wet with oil as it made a wavy path from his forehead to his ear. His black patent leather shoes didn't have a speck of dust. He couldn't have been more perfectly dressed. Her eyes travelled up his body taking inventory of every button and fold until her eyes rested on his face. His pale white skin had a blue tinge as though he had never been in the sun a day in his life. The line of his jaw was sharp and sculpted. Prominent cheek bones and a high forehead. He was everything mother had every told her about fine lineage. He stopped inches away from her and held out his elbow waiting. She looked at it and then up into his pale blue eyes, blue like the sky on a hazy cloudy day when you can't tell if it's blue or just a shade of cool white. He stood as still as stone waiting, looking into her eyes. At this moment, it was her choice. She could flee or she could take his arm. He waited for her to choose. She wondered about the risks of choosing to hook her hand around his elbow. Accepting his protection from a loose pebble that could trip her seemed a small concession, but did he see it as more. Did he take it as her relinquishing herself to him?

She decided she was over-thinking it and slipped her hand around his elbow. A smile curled around the side of his mouth. He was pleased with this first step. She, on the other hand, had conflicting flashes of heat and fear that he truly did take that as winning another pawn in the chess game that ended with him owning her.

His restraint and chivalrous posture gave her the feeling she was royalty being escorted inside. He held his arm out, fixed like petrified wood. He didn't take any liberties to try to hug her or touch her. There was a coldness, but there was also strength. She decided the coldness was not truly lack of emotion, but rather her looking at him through modern eyes. A man from her time would have put his hand on her, either around her waist or her shoulders, yet Brian was trying very hard to keep a distance.

Inside, she could see the obvious difference between this house and Bettie's. Bettie had some nice things, but her house reminded her more of historic homes she had visited where people had actually lived there. Brian's house looked like a palace inside. Marble floors greeted them at the door and flowed seamlessly with the marble columns of the foyer. A marble stairway swept up around the curve of the wall and disappeared into the ceiling. In the center of the foyer was a round table with a centerpiece of twisted grape vines with red flowers tucked into the twists. The flowers looked odd to her, or rather out of season.

"Where did you get these flowers in the dead of winter?" she asked.

"My mother grows them in the conservatory. They are native to France, brought here by ship in a glass terrarium."

"Oh. They are lovely." She leaned in to smell their fragrance.

His lips curled up in the corners again showing he was pleased she liked them. He reached out and took a blossom from its crevice and tucked the short stem behind her braid next to the French twist of her bun. Admiring her, he took her hand and kissed the back of her knuckles.

"Your beauty is only matched by the wonder of God's flowers."

The heat crept up her neck slowly engulfing her face. She knew she had a full-fledged blush.

"Oh Brian, how lovely. Your guest has arrived. I have been looking forward to meeting you Miss Wallingsford." A handsome woman about her mother's age floated into the foyer and stopped in front of them.

"Yes, Momma. This is Miss Lily Wallingsford of Frankfort." Turning to Lily. "May I present my mother, Mrs. Charles Everbright."

Lily was not sure what the appropriate response should be. She decided a bobbing curtsy was probably best and attempted one as gracefully as she could. It seemed to please Mrs. Everbright who nodded approvingly.

"It's a pleasure to meet you, ma'am," she added.

"Yes, yes, and you, too, dear. It's so good of you to take on the students of Stephensport on such short notice and apparently on your retreat from your duties in Frankfort."

"Yes, well, it's no problem."

"Brian, dear, would you see what's keeping your father? I would love a chance to get to know our guest better."

97

Brian bowed apologetically to her and left the room.

"Now, dear, let's sit, shall we?" She motioned toward a blue velvet settee' near a fireplace with a low fire. Lily sat with her body turned slightly toward the older woman. She could feel the soft heat of the fireplace on her arm.

"Mrs. Everbright, your home is beautiful."

Mrs. Everbright waved off the compliment as though that fact was a given. "Yes, well, Charley likes it. Personally, I would rather be back in New York. I miss the city."

Lily could not imagine that whatever home they had in New York could have been any nicer than this. She must be homesick.

"How long has your family been in Kentucky?" Lily asked.

"It's been five years. Charles followed the McCracken brothers here when they decided to make their fortune in the wilderness. He figured if it was good enough for them, it was good enough for us. After all, someone has to sell them nice clothes."

"Wilderness," Lily repeated, mulling over the comparison to New York.

She noticed the pale cream crepe dress Mrs. Everbright wore. Small folds of fabric on the bodice had pearl beads sewn into them with green and maroon embroidered flowers and leaves. A maroon velvet ribbon circled the neckline and made a collar. Her whitening blond hair was swept up into waves and held by delicate combs encrusted with tiny pearls. The pearls were the same color as her hair so that you would have missed them if you weren't sitting this close and looking.

"So, do you have other children besides Brian?"

Her mouth rose in a sweet smile but her eyes didn't share the sentiment, "Yes. I have a daughter. She is still in New York. I miss Eva very much."

"I see. She doesn't get to visit much?"

"No. But do tell me about Frankfort and your family."

"Frankfort is pretty in the spring time. Redbuds bloom first after the long winter with pinkish purple buds. There is a great deal of rock in the hillsides which you can see when there is no foliage. The wet limestone and purple buds make it a beautiful place that time of year."

"That sounds lovely."

"I live with my mom and dad. Dad is a state worker."

Mrs. Everbright's forehead crinkled up with confusion.

"I mean, he works at the capitol. He works in a lawyer's office in the capitol."

"Oh! I see. Do you see Governor Buckner or his wife much?"

"Hm, no. I don't. I guess I'm just very busy with teaching, you know."

"I see. He seems most disagreeable to me. Vetoing everything. Personally, I am hoping John Young Brown is successful in his bid to succeed him. I think he would do great things for this state."

Lily tried to remember if this Governor Brown was related to the governor by the same name that served Kentucky in the 1980s. Surely not, but how coincidental would that be to have the same name.

"I guess so. I'm not as familiar with him."

"Oh my, I am boring you to tears with talk of politics, aren't I? So, tell me what you like about teaching?"

Lily was glad she changed the subject. "I really like getting to know my students and helping them find what motivates them to learn."

99

Now it was Mrs. Everbright's turn to look like a fish out of water. She stared at her and blinked. "Isn't their motivation to keep from getting in trouble?"

"Yes and no. I don't find that fear of punishment is the best motivator for helping students develop a love of learning."

"A love of learning? I don't know of any students who love to learn. Well, you must be very good at what you do. Lord knows, if you can make those hooligans love learning, you'll be the best teacher I have ever seen."

"I find that students are naturally curious and with guidance, that can push them to learn more successfully than just memorizing."

"Memorizing is a key part of school." The male voice startled Lily and she jumped to turn around in her seat. Brian had been listening at the doorway. "Mother, father will be down in a moment."

It's not that Lily had never heard anyone extoll the virtues of memorization. There had been plenty of parents that complained that she didn't send home more homework to give their kids a chance to memorize facts on a study guide. It's how they had been taught to learn and they saw no problem with it. In fact, they saw a problem with her because they thought she was too soft not giving more drills and repetitive homework.

She was of the opinion that children needed to play after school. They needed time to discover what thrilled them by exploring their world. Making them sit to do repetitive drills after school defeated the play/learn mental process. There was no modern research that proved thirty minutes of drill at home tacked onto the school day made a hill of beans difference. One thing that had been proven was that adding play time into the school day improved test scores. More creative play exercised the mind. It taught it to reason, imagine, predict and reflect. Those were all the things she wanted her students to do at school.

Naturally students needed guidance to apply those skills to be become educated, but without play, the students had no idea what she was trying to get them to do. The one thing she didn't have to teach them was to dream. As long as that had not been squashed out of them, as it apparently had been with the girls, she could guide them to apply what they already knew how to do to what they had never thought of before.

That was true learning, not stuffing random facts in their brain that could be regurgitated. Without the ability to process the facts, facts were useless knowledge.

"Mr. Everbright, have you had any training in education theory?"

"No. No, I haven't, but I know what it takes to be successful in life."

"Of course you do. You are a successful business man. Did you learn everything you needed to know about business in grammar school?"

He glared at her now. She could tell he did not like being questioned. "Obviously not. I worked with my father in his store after school. But I could not have learned to run the business if I didn't know how to write and do arithmetic."

"But you do agree that teaching every student to read and do arithmetic will not make them all successful business men?"

"Of course. I also like to think business acumen runs in my blood. Not all students have that advantage."

"Oh, I agree. There are different abilities that make a great difference. What I'm saying is that being taught how to think, by applying skills all children naturally have at their disposal, would give all students a chance to be successful at anything for which they have an advantage."

He didn't speak right away, thinking it over. Finally, he raised his chin so that he looked down his nose at her. "My dear, many of those students will never have any advantage. Their lot is to plow the ground or make stew and produce squalling new students who will do the same as their fathers and mothers. Filling their heads with useless thoughts and dreams only hinders them. It's cruel, really. Many of the students in our school have no business even being there. I don't subscribe to the whole 'education for all' mantra, but that's what is expected these days."

With a wave of nausea, she felt like a brick was lodged in her stomach. She had surely found the most backward-minded education administrator that ever existed. Faced with someone so diametrically different in education philosophy stumped her. Worse yet, this was her boss. If she was going to follow her instincts about how to proceed, she would have to do it without letting him know.

"Then I will have to help them become the best farmers, stew makers and squalling baby producers they can be," she offered.

He and Mrs. Everbright both looked at her trying to figure out her statement. It had a sharp edge, to be sure.

Finally, the butler broke the awkward silence by announcing that dinner was served. The ladies got up and they all filed into the hallway. The dining room did not fail to impress her. The Gilded Age loved the Sun King. Louis the XIV would have felt right at home. Golden side boards with marble tops held silver tourines and platters of delicacies. The long table with silver, china and crystal settings was crowned with a chandelier that was nearly as big as the table. Lavish picture frames held portraits of grumpy elders gracing the walls. Every meal was a family reunion with their disapproving eyes.

Brian pulled out an upholstered chair with golden silk fabric for her. She sat and he scooted it forward before the footman pulled out a chair for him. He sat at the end of the table nearest to her. At the other end of the table sat his mother in the mirror image place of Lily. The seat at the far end of the table was vacant.

Lily waited patiently for a clue as to what to do next. She knew manners at this time were strict and unforgiving. She hoped that if she just did whatever Mrs. Everbright did, she would be alright. The door to the hallway opened and an older gentleman appeared walking straight in. He didn't seem to take any notice of them. His clothing was impeccable. Dark tuxedo with a vest and detachable collar with wings. A black silk tie was tucked into the vest. The jacket appeared small compared to the boxy suits of the modern time. Even his coat sleeves seemed too short. It made his upper body look small to her. It was the style of the time, though, she knew. It reminded her of a photo of Charlie Chaplin she'd seen.

The footman pulled out his chair and he turned to sit down. Now that she had a chance to get a good look at him, she could see the similarity of the two men. Brian was certainly more handsome, but the hooked nose, the gray-blue eyes, and the ability to stare into your soul came from the male line. His mother's chiseled jawline and perfect skin gave Brian an edge above his father in looks.

"Miss Wallingsford, I presume," he bellowed staring at her. "Welcome. Very good of you to join us for dinner."

"Thank you for the invitation. It's a pleasure to be here," she offered back.

Mrs. Everbright smiled slightly and Lily had to wonder if it was her idea or Brian's to invite her. She seemed so gracious.

"As I am also on the Town Council, I am aware of your credentials for teaching. We are fortunate to have you in the interim while we search for a replacement for Miss Smith."

"Thank you. I'll do my best." She really didn't feel comfortable making small talk. She worried she was going to say something outside of the protocols of etiquette. However, she realized that if she didn't ask a question, the conversation was going to quickly turn to her. "So, tell me about the clothing business? Where do you shop for inventory?"

Dinner proceeded as she hoped with Mr. Everbright, the senior, educating her about the challenges of the fashion business. She found it surprisingly fascinating despite never having given one wit about fashion or clothes. All in all, they were very gracious to her. She may have made several social blunders, but there was no gasping or raised eyebrows.

The server brought dessert and set it in front of her. A small dish of bread pudding. The aroma of hot nutmeg tickled her nose. Little chunks of bread with browned corners and a sprinkling of raisins filled the dish. It didn't look like the bread pudding she had seen that was swimming in an egg colored gravy. She had never seen the appeal of the plain, gooey dish. This, however, looked like a precious cake made of an ordinary food now dressed up for a fancy table. The sweet raisins and warm nutmeg filled her with anticipation for something special.

She spooned a bit into her mouth and was filled with the warm feeling of family, home, memories of Christmas.

"This is delicious. I've never tasted a bread pudding this good."

"You are such a dear. I'll certainly let cook know you enjoyed it," Mrs. Everbright beamed. The footman and butler stood along the wall staring forward like soldiers.

After dinner, they retired to the parlor. Brian took her to a far side of the room to talk. His parents chatted and sipped something in a small goblet.

"Miss Wallingsford, have you enjoyed our company?" he asked.

"Oh, yes. You're all very kind. Thank you."

"I'm glad. They're not too bad." He nodded his head in his parent's direction. "I must say, you are the most beautiful woman I have ever seen." His eyes traveled across her shoulder, down the hem of her dress across her bosom and then back up her neck to her face. The effect was almost as stunning as if he had traced the route with his fingers. She realized she'd stopped breathing and was having a hard time loosening herself from the moment to take a breath. She should have been annoyed by his obvious flirtation but the look in his eyes held her mind from any rational thought.

In a wave of sanity that returned her to her senses, self-doubt blew air in her lungs, "I hardly believe that."

"It's very good that my parents are just a few yards away. Otherwise, I could not hope to restrain myself. I cannot deny what you do to me, Miss Wallingsford."

Still perplexed by his infatuation, she decided to make him unpack it, "I don't understand why, exactly. I know there are very beautiful ladies in this town. I have seen them. And, I while I know I am not unsightly, I'm no beauty queen."

He closed his eyes and exhaled. "Yes, I do find you easy to look at, a beautiful queen, as you say, however, your intrigue comes from inside. There is a way about you which I do not see with the girls here. I can't put my finger on it. It's a confidence or assuredness. Whatever it is, I just want to drink it in and, well, love you. I want to love every inch of your skin. "

"Mr. Everbright!" She was shocked at his forwardness. Such confessions could ruin their working relationship. "I'm not sure it's appropriate for- for my boss to say such things." She knew sexual harassment laws were a hundred years in the making, but hopefully he would take her seriously.

"Your boss." He hung his head and shook it. "I've never heard a woman talk about a man as her boss. I don't see it that way at all. I supervise several clerks at the store. They are good men. But you are not like them. Teachers are like sisters I care about. For you, however, I have much more passionate thoughts than one would have for a sister."

He took her hand in his and rubbed a circle on the back of her hand with his thumb. The smooth softness of his skin pressing warmth into her made her want to melt. She could all too easily imagine his warm fingers exploring places that never get touched. Places that are ticklish from lack of touch. She was losing her focus. She reminded herself this was her boss. Being entangled with him would make it very difficult to have a professional relationship. A nagging thought tickled her brain. It was the way he thought of her. He wasn't just a boss that fell for her. It hit her all at once: he never thought of her as a professional. All women were potential romantic interests to him. Her career was of no importance to him.

"Dearest Lily, I must admit, I have very strong feelings for you that I cannot ignore. You thrill me."

Here she was sitting in front of a man that made her feel like Cinderella dancing with the prince, but this Cinderella was a professional housekeeper and was proud of it. She'd be darned if she was going to give up her career for a block-headed Victorian man.

She covered a pretend yawn. "Please don't take it the wrong way, but I am so tired. I need to go home."

He jerked back to reality, "Certainly. Let me call for the carriage and your coat."

"Thank you," she said feeling in control.

He stood and offered his hand to help her up. She said goodbye to Mr. and Mrs. Everbright, thanking them for a lovely evening while Brian called for the carriage. He walked her to the door and helped her get her jacket on. She just wanted to get out to have time to process her thoughts. They were waiting for the driver to stick his head in to alert them he was there.

"Miss Wallingsford, There's a ball at an associate's in Union Star next Saturday. My parents are going and could chaperone." He paused, "Would you come as my guest?"

"I, uh, I didn't pack a ball gown. I didn't expect to need one." That was the truth, she thought.

He smiled a warm smile of triumph, "My dear, you will never be lacking for something beautiful to wear as long as I'm in your favor. Come by the store this week and pick out anything you fancy. It's my gift for accepting my invitation."

A girl could get used to words like that, she thought. Suddenly she couldn't remember why she had wanted to leave so soon. "Uh, alright then, I would love to."

If a man could bubble up with happiness, that's what he did. He held her hands in his and pulled her close to him. For a brief moment, his lips hovered over hers. She wanted to back up, but her body betrayed her. She could smell the nutmeg on his breath. She closed her eyes and all the warmth of home with the exhilaration of wanting him swirled in her mind. She felt the heat of his lips on hers and froze on the spot, letting him do as he pleased. She wanted him to. She wanted him to have her. She wanted to let go of herself and give all that she was to him. He pressed in and held her firmly, squeezing. Then in a burst of passion, ravenously kissed her deeply.

The sound of laughter in the parlor distracted him, and just as quickly as he'd stolen the kiss, he stood up straight as though nothing had happened. It had happened, though, and she could see in his eyes that he was slightly undone. He gritted his teeth and held his face expressionless. She straightened, too, and pursed her lips, mad at herself. She didn't want to want him.

The driver opened the door and let them know he was there. Brian escorted her to the carriage and helped her inside. Then he pulled himself into the carriage as well. Apparently, he was escorting her home. At first she felt annoyed because she needed to think about how she felt, but when she looked over at the driver and darkness of the winter night, she realized how vulnerable she felt. At least with him there, she felt safe.

"Thank you for accepting my invitation. Your company will linger on my mind." Taking her hand, he kissed her knuckles. "I shall come by the Black's for you on the day of the ball."

She already regretted telling him she would go. The carriage lurched forward. His thigh rubbed against her leg as the carriage jostled them. Their clothes did nothing to stop the heat that radiated off him. She could feel his muscled leg pressing against her. She closed her eyes trying to keep her mind from sinking into the base lust that was consuming her. The taste of his lips was fresh in her memory. Forceful, passionate kisses promising her unrelenting attention crowded her thoughts. Feeling dizzy, she opened her eyes to find him watching her with a satisfied smile. He knew he had made the impact he wanted to make. She could tell by his look that he was pleased with the evening. He had her right where he wanted her and he didn't even realize how different they were. She knew, and she hated herself for the betrayal of her body to her mind.

"I would love to be inside your mind. The look on your face just now was bliss. I do hope you were thinking of me."

His charm was undeniable. It was the only excuse for why she could find him so attractive and yet want to punch him at the same time. There was no way this would be a good match for her. She would never be able to make him see her point of view. Yet, she ached for his touch. She wanted to feel his arms around her and nestle her head in his chest. She knew that to be his would be to be safe, cared for, and never want for anything. It seemed that even his love would freely be hers. It was everything she had wanted. Both what her mother had tried to find and what she herself wanted. Brian Everbright surely must be perfect for her. But if this was the case, why did she have to fight back the urge to jump from the carriage and run.

She knew the reason. Despite everything in his favor on her personal checklist, she knew he would put no stock in her career. In fact, he was the one obstacle, even now, to what she wanted to do with the school girls of Stephensport. Her career never entered his mind because, to him, women didn't have careers. She should feel glad to accept all he offered in his mind. In fact, nearly every woman of this time would agree with him.

"Miss Wallingsford, are you feeling quite well?" He furrowed his brow with worry.

"Oh, certainly. I was just thinking."

"Thinking? You truly are a mystery. Quite intriguing, I say. Your face seemed much too serious just now to be thinking of me. Are you worried about your honor? It's true we should not be sharing the inside of the carriage. I assure you, you are quite safe. If you would feel better, I would be happy to ride with the driver."

She giggled at that. He actually thought she was worried for her safety. Then it occurred to her that she probably should be worried. She had been out on numerous dates alone with men and rarely ever worried about her honor.

"No, I feel very safe. I was just thinking about school—"

He cut her off, "Now don't fret. If you need time off to get your dress or take care of matters of beauty, just let me know."

Her expression was frozen after the word school as she tried to imagine that he was so unaware of her dilemma that he thought she was worried about time to get her hair done before the ball.

In a whim to create a little drama and slow down Brian's forward progress, blurted out a statement meant to distract Brian. "Well, I'm not sure about my plans for the date of the ball. Evan McEwen asked me to accompany him to a picnic and I need to check my calendar."

"Evan McEwen!" His eyebrows shot up in obvious frustration. "Not to be blunt, my dearest, but surely a man like that shouldn't be worthy of your time. Why on earth would you entertain his vulgar attempts at attention when I am seeking it?"

She wasn't sure what to say and sat there with her mouth open for a minute. "A girl has to keep all her options open. Surely you understand."

"No. I am not certain you are thinking straight."

They didn't speak any more on the way home which suited Lily just fine.

The horses slowed and they came to a stop. Brian jumped down first and then lifted her out of the carriage. Again, he offered his arm and stoically led her to the door. The door opened before they made it to the doorstep and William stepped out.

"Thank you for taking good care of our guest," William offered. "Would you care to join me in the parlor for nightcap, Mr. Everbright?"

"Very kind of you to offer, but I must be getting home."

The two men bowed slightly and William held the door for Lily as she went in. Brian turned and went back to his carriage. Evan watched from the corner of the porch. He sat in the shadows watching. After Brian's carriage was out of sight, he blew out a deep exhale. The cool night air stung his lungs but not as badly as the stinging in his heart. With every fiber of his being, he hated Brian Everbrig

Chapter 6 – The Desire of a Heart

Lily stood at her window staring at the darkness. She could almost pretend it was 2018 and she was staying at a historical inn, just like she planned when she left Frankfort. She missed home. She missed her mom and dad. She missed her students. She brought their young faces up in her mind and traced the curves of their cheeks. For eight hours a day, they were her kids. She couldn't help but love them like her own. She protected them, reminded them to wear a coat, made sure they ate, and worried about them when they weren't with her. Most had good families but for some she knew school was break from the heartbreak at home.

She wondered if time had carried on in 2018. Would a substitute take over for her? Where search crews out? Would they search for her abandoned car? Or, had time stopped? Was it frozen in the future, not yet created. If she never made it back, would some other teacher fill her place in her students' lives? Who would brush and braid Natalie's hair because her mother was never home? Would they know Adam didn't mean to seem disrespectful but just had to put up a shield to protect his heart? Would they know Tyler wanted more than anything to please her and needed an encouraging word to keep him from giving up?

While all that weighed on her, a nagging emotion skirted the edges of her mind. She had been alone in 2018. Now she had two men wooing her. Two very different men, but neither seemed very interested in her career. Neither Evan nor Brian would want her to continue teaching if she married them. They needed her to fulfill a role. Perhaps Brian needed her less than Evan but his views of education would stifle her dreams.

"Grandma, if you managed to orchestrate this time-travel fiasco, why did you have to send me somewhere where two Mr. Wrongs wanted me?" she whispered out loud.

Silence replaced her words. Nothing. Why did she travel back in time? What if it was just a fluke freak accident with no real reason at all? Maybe she could just remain single but change education back before public education even gets going. What would education be like if she changed history? Then again, how could she go up against an ingrained culture that subjugated girls? After all, she certainly wouldn't be the first woman to try to change the world. As satisfying as trying to change the world would be, wouldn't her life her be just as lonely as it was in 2018?

She pressed her eyes shut trying to block out the world. Crawling in bed, she wished she could hide under her hand-stitched quilt forever. She wrapped her arms around herself. The soft, satiny skin of her arms felt good on her fingertips. She caressed her bicep, imagining what Evan would think if he was doing it. She imagined how she would feel. The muscles of her core contracted in a luxurious grip and she stretched her legs, pointing her toes to stretch her belly. She sighed deeply. There was no doubt about it, Brian Everbright had a great deal to offer, but Evan was who she craved.

Like a hot, golden honey emotion, being desired for the woman she was by a man who knew how to love her was a fantasy she could not shake. It was not practical or safe, but there was nothing lonely about it.

***

Evan walked a path in the woods by moonlight trying to calm the restlessness in his nerves. The thought of Lily in Brian's company made his blood pressure rise like the humming of bees in a hive. He could hear his pulse in his ears. There was no way he could get in bed and drift off to sleep. He certainly couldn't stay near the main house knowing she was a few steps away.

He wanted to run up the stairs and grab her by the shoulders and talk some sense into her. He could tell though, that she was not a woman that would take kindly to an authoritative tone. It had seemed so simple before. He hoped to woo her into allowing him to court her, accepting his hand in marriage and they would begin a life of farming and child raising together. She was a woman he could look at day in and day out and never get tired of. It seemed so practical, but then she accepted Mr. Everbright's invitation to dinner. Somehow this hit him like a thief stealing what belonged to him. Who did he think he was? Were there not enough shallow, useless mannequins that man could hang on his arm at parties?

There was something different about Lily. She seemed to take on teaching as though it were a mission, not just a job to be done to fill in and fill her time. She truly cared about her students even though it had only been two days. He watched her sit in the parlor and think. She seemed to be planning and problem-solving. Women he knew would busy themselves with the task at hand to get through it and move on. Life was easy to them. They would do what was required and then pass the time resting. Lily thought like a man as though life had more meaning than today. In fact, most men he knew were not much different than the woman. He had dreamed and planned to move to America. He took a big risk leaving everything behind and set out from the safety of his family.

She had the same passion for life. The thought of holding a woman with dreams and the drive to reach them excited him and scared him at the same time. What if she didn't put him and children as a priority? Would she be able to do the work a woman must do and still follow whatever dreams she had? How would he be able to help her reach those dreams?

The answers were out of reach but he couldn't deny she rocked him to the core. He wanted to hold her and breathe the scent of her skin. He longed to hear her tell him she loved him. He thought of whispering that he loved her in her ear and her smiling with joy.

He came to a bluff over the river. Below, the mighty Ohio quietly ambled toward the Mississippi on its journey to be free of all land and pour into the Gulf of Mexico. These hills were passing obstacles on its journey.

He sat in the moonlight, knees drawn up and held by his clasped hands. A light breeze ruffled his hair. The white light reflected off the water like a shining ribbon streaming through blackness. The serene beauty of the silent body of water was deceptive. He knew that the churning currents would take a man under and hold him down. Catfish as large as a cow hide in the dark depths. River fish with razor teeth waited under the surface for an easy meal. Life, like this beautiful view, was deceptive.

What he thought he had always wanted, may not actually be what he needed. He'd moved to America to have land

and wealth and a family. At no point had he considered his heart. His heart did not care about land and wealth. He just wanted Lily. He wanted her with every fiber of his being. Like a magnet, he could sense her in the wilderness below. She was there at the base of the hill, at the end of the road, in the house just before Sinking Creek. There in a room upstairs in the back of the house. Her spirit radiated out to him in the night from her bed.

Or, did it radiate out to Brian Everbright? He knew any sensible girl would chose Brian Everbright over him. After all, survival was primal. The Everbrights had money. She would never worry about food. She would never go to bed bone tired from the sweat of her brow.

He grimaced. What did he have to offer her? He couldn't bear it. He couldn't sit back and watch Brian Everbright picking her up and dropping her off. One day she would come home with a ring. He would have to attend their wedding.

His heart pounded, spreading the ache in his chest to every inch of him. Maybe if he had been the first born at home, he could have competed with the likes of Brian Everbright for Lily's love. He had to leave Scotland and cross an ocean to find a life and now he knew it didn't matter. Heartache went with him everywhere he went. One thing was for certain. He was not going to sit back and watch the woman he loved, the woman for whom he would give up everything, become another man's wife. He was leaving. He'd follow the glistening stream of silver below him and, together, he and the river would find freedom.

***

The dim light of dawn made a gray cast on the room when her eyes opened. The sounds of dishes and pans

116

clanging somewhere in the house woke her. The aroma of coffee pulled at her, begging her to find it. She sat up on the side of the bed and stretched, pulling her hands high over her head. As she stretched, she noticed a green dress hanging on the wardrobe door. Bettie must have left it there earlier.

She quickly dressed, becoming more adept at tightening her own corset, and washed her face from the wash basin on the dresser. She brushed her hair until it shined with a golden glow in the low light and pinned it back up using the combs to pull it up on the sides before twisting it into a bun in the back.

In the kitchen, Bettie bustled from the stove to the table setting out bowls of oatmeal, sausage and biscuits. William sat at the table reading the newspaper and Carlton sipped a glass of milk.

"Anything I can do to help, Bettie?" Lily asked.

"Just sit down, darling. That'll be fine. You can pour yourself some coffee."

Lily picked up the china coffee server and poured herself a cup. She added two lumps of sugar and stirred it with a spoon. Before laying the spoon down, her eyes fell on a small crystal vase on the table with a few sprigs of cedar with pale blue berries dotting the faded green spray of leaves. The scent of them now wafted by her nose. The sharp woody scent reminded her of a cedar chest. The flat evergreen leaves tickled her memory and then she froze. The memory gripped her.

She replayed the moment in her mind where she had sat at her grandmother's grave and tucked a sprig of cedar with the little pale berries into a bobby pin holding her hair back. She remembered the scent perfectly. In that instant she knew it clear as anything: the cedar sprig was what sent her back in time.

117

"What're you looking at, Miss Wallingsford?" Carlton asked studying her.

She looked up at him as though surprised she was not alone. Time revved forward again and she realized she was touching the stem of leaves in the vase. "I don't know. It's just, this sprig," she paused. "It smells nice." She stalled trying to get her head back.

Bettie sat a butter plate and cream pitcher on the table, "Thank you, honeycakes. They were on the table when I came in this morning. I suppose Mr. McMcEwen left them. He grinds them into a soap that he likes to use."

"Oh. Sure. Of course." Lily was putting the pieces together in her head. The coincidence of all these facts swirled in her mind.

"William, have you seen Evan this morning?" Bettie asked.

"No, ma'am."

"It's not like him to be late for breakfast."

"I'm sure he'll be along. He probably went to check the animals."

Bettie looked out the kitchen window on her way back to the stove. "Well, go ahead and get started. You all need to be on your way."

Lily ate some oatmeal. Something about cedar trees kept nagging at her. When she was finished, she excused herself and quickly pulled her jacket on and headed out the door.

The morning air was cool and crisp with frost making the grass look fuzzy. She scanned the tall hilltop of the cemetery. The tall cedar trees swayed in the cold wind. A memory of a field trip came to mind. She and the students had gone to an Indian reenactment of sorts and heard of a legend of the cedar tree. She wracked her brain to remember and then it dawned on her. The legend goes that the spirits

118

of ancestors are held in the tree. It was becoming more apparent that somehow that cedar sprig had to be involved in her time travel.

She walked up Main Street to the church that served as the school and went inside. She opened the door to the stove and stuffed kindling inside and placed two small logs on top of it. The she dragged a match over the top of the stove and used it to light the kindling. She closed the stove door and shook out the match. It was too cool to take her coat off. To keep from shivering, she grabbed a broom and started working it over the floor, sweeping dust and debris into a small pile.

"Miss Wallinsford?" a soft voice called out.

Lily spun around to see Priscilla standing in the doorway. A cold draft rolled through the schoolhouse and blanketed Lily's feet. "Close the door, honey. Come in."

"Priscilla closed the door carefully and turned, "Are you sure it's okay I came early?"

"Sure it is. Do you want to talk about something?"

"No ma'am. I was just thinking, I can get to school early and not be missed. Maybe you could teach me to write letters before school instead of after."

"What a marvelous idea! Of course! Let's get to work!"

***

Lily felt good about the day. She thought about it on the short walk home. Priscilla took to writing like a duck to water. She'd given her some work to do at home on a tablet and Priscilla beamed with delight that she would soon know how to write like her brothers.

She counted the boys off in teams and put them to work on a project to design a water wheel that would work even in a drought. At first they seemed lost. They had never

119

worked in teams, much less on work where they had to set the rules. The room was buzzing with the teams' conversations.

While the boys were busy, she had the girls come to the carpet to talk about what they had dreamed of doing. One of the young girls said she wondered if there was a way to make wings on a wagon so that if it fell off a cliff, it would glide to the bottom. He eyes crinkled with delight as she described them and Lily couldn't help but think of Amelia Earhart. Perhaps Amelia's mother was given permission to dream and raised a daughter that dreamed as well. Lily's heart filled with hope as it occurred to her that these girls could change history, or they could influence future generations, if they could open their minds a little.

That afternoon, she walked home lost in her thoughts. The house was quiet when she came in the front door. In the foyer, she unbuttoned her coat and started to shimmy out of the narrow cuffs. All was eerily quiet. She shrugged the coat off and carried it into the kitchen. The breakfast dishes sat in the sink. Something was wrong.

"Bettie! William!" She paused waiting. "Carlton! Evan!"
No response.

She burst out the back door. A chicken pecked at the dried grass near the house making clucking noises. She glanced back to the barn. The door was open. She ran toward it. Something had to be terribly wrong. She hoped no one was hurt.

The wagon was gone and Bettie sat on a wood crate holding Carlton who was crying quietly into her coat.

"What's the matter?" she breathed.

"Evan is gone. His bed wasn't slept in. All his things are gone. William is looking for him."

Lily felt her breath leave her and not come back. He left. How could he do that? He took himself away from her. She'd mistakenly thought she had time to choose.

Reasons presented themselves in her mind: he'd gotten a better job, there was an opportunity to own land, there was another girl, and lastly, what she knew was the real truth, he didn't want her. Just like Andrew, he didn't want her. It was all a show to see if she would take the bait and then he ran. Perhaps it was worse. Perhaps he was mad at her for seeing Brian. He hadn't wanted her to. She didn't think it was unfair of her. They weren't promised or engaged. Whatever the reason, he had pulled himself out and was gone. Part of her felt hollow. She knew it now, though it hadn't been clear before, he'd taken part of her heart with him.

She turned around so Bettie wouldn't see the tears. She was startled when Bettie's hand touched her shoulder.

"Lily, are you well?"

Lily pulled a handkerchief from her skirt pocket and dried her tears. "Yeah." She turned to face Bettie, "Do you all have any idea where he went?"

"No. William has been out looking all day. He has some friends looking as well. It appears that he willingly left because his bag and what few clothes he had are gone as well."

Lily stood motionless taking it in.

"Oh, honey." Bettie put her arms around her and squeezed. "I see that your heart is torn."

Lily nodded as the sound met her ears of a horse clopping the ground as it pulled the wagon around the house. William sat alone in the seat of the buckboard wagon. A cloud of dust kicked up from the commotion. William's face looked grim.

The wagon slowed and William jumped from the seat. In two strides, he stood beside them.

121

"William, dear, tell us some news." Bettie clasped her hands in front of her silently pleading for good news.

"After searching all over, we finally heard a dock hand say a man by his description boarded a steamboat at dawn that was carrying cargo downriver." He paused and kicked at the dirt. "It sure looks like he left on his own accord. I just wish he'd told us so we wouldn't have worried."

"Why would he do it?" Bettie asked.

"No telling, honeycakes." He took her hand. "But he chose it and we have to respect it."

William and Bettie turned to Lily. She couldn't breathe. Shock quickly turned to anger and she pursed her lips. Pain tore at her heart, burning from the inside. He'd taken himself from her and there was nothing she could do.

"His loss!" She turned from them and set out toward the house to get away from their searching stares. She walked away and didn't look back at them. She didn't want to face them. She could hear them talking but her mind was spinning.

She made it to the back door and held the door casing to steady herself. Dizziness threatened to take her down. Hot tears and anger welled up. She squeezed her eyes tightly shut refusing to let the emotion loose. Betraying her, tears fell in big drops as she rested her head on her arms on the door casing.

She risked a glance back and saw Bettie and William still standing by the barn watching her and whispering to each other. The furrows in Bettie's brow told her they werc worried. Worried about her and worried about Evan.

She turned the doorknob and darted into the kitchen. Everything looked like a scene in a museum. The iron stove took up a large portion of the kitchen. Cast iron skillets with cold grease caked in the bottom. A small glass front cabinet

122

held china plates. They were thick and sturdy. A water pump stood over the large sink next to a counter. A sack of flour sat on the counter and flour was spread in front of it. A rolling pin waited for Bettie's hands to put it to work.

The kitchen was probably very similar to the one at Brian Everbright's house. The difference was that the Blacks used the kitchen for every meal. The kitchen was the heart of the home. Life happened here. Bettie cooked, William talked to her, and Evan sat at the simple worn wooden table and renewed his strength with the bounty Bettie created with her hands.

The Blacks weren't as poor as some of the children at the school, but they weren't upper crust, either. They were as close to middle class as you could get in this time. The absence of servants excluded them from the elusive upper class, but William built Bettie a house with all the rooms an elite family would need, which let them waffle in the middle of the class system.

She remembered that Bettie had come from a wealthy family. She had been used to having nice things in a nice home. She'd even had servants. Even so, she didn't seem bothered by her life now. Growing up, she'd been served food that a cook prepared. Her mother had not cooked and neither had she, but now Bettie had to cook all the meals, clean the house and everything else.

Even now, with her heart aching from Evan's absence, she wondered if she would be smarter to give Brian her attention. She groaned at herself. It seemed that the problems of her life in the future were just amplified here. The urge to find Evan started with a tug in her chest. In this time, it would be so unreasonable for her to chase him. She surely couldn't go alone, but worse than that, women absolutely did not chase after men.

She pushed back the urge and closed a door on it. She couldn't think about it, even though she knew there was more to that urge than missing the goosebumps he gave her.

Her eyes fell on the small vase with the cedar sprig still on the table. She plucked it out of the water and held it in front of her.

"So you did this, huh?"

The sprig sagged limply and one of small berries fell to the floor. She lifted the sprig to her nose and breathed in the scent. What used to remind her of Christmas or visiting her grandmother's grave now only left her with a vision of Evan. The scent of his skin permeating through his work shirt filled her mind.

She yelled at the sprig, "Send me home!" Tears sprang to her eyes as sobs gripped her. It was all too much. A confining culture, a new body, men who boldly pursued her, and now the realization that somehow a cedar sprig could send her through time overwhelmed her senses.

***

Evan stood on the deck of the steam boat watching the paddle wheel turn. The sound of water falling through the paddles reminded him of the ocean waves crashing on the shore of his village in Scotland. That home seemed so far away now. Too far to ever get back. Now he was traveling again. The pain of loss in his heart now was the same as leaving Scotland: leaving those he loved.

The river bank was so far from the boat, the people working their riverbank farms looked like toys silently feeding horses, putting away plows and taking down laundry from a line. They had the life he always wanted. Husbands and wives working together for a common good on their land. He watched the woman in a long skirt reaching to unclip the sheets. She seemed content, but what if she wasn't? What if she had dreamed of doing other things with her life? He had always been free to pursue his dreams no matter where that led him, but what was the lot of women. He had never really considered their dreams. It was so easy as a man to assume their dreams were of home and children.

What if, as a young woman, they had other dreams? Their fathers set them up for a marriage they may or may not want and their dreams get pushed aside. He tried to imagine if he had been forced to stay in Scotland playing second fiddle to his brother. It struck him how unfair it would be to be female.

Lily's face filled his mind. She was a perfect example of a woman that had dreams. He could tell she wanted more than a home and children. Would it be fair of him to force her to live his dreams at the expense of hers? But, how would it work? How could they both get what they want out of life? He couldn't imagine how that would work.

He turned away from the shoreline and leaned against the rail. The steamboat had traveled all day since dawn and approached the merging with the Mississippi River. The sun hung low in the sky in a burst of dark orange that made all the bare black branches of hibernating trees stand out. As the current pulled the big boat a smidge faster, he felt a zing of exhilaration. It felt good to get away from his pain. Then the thought occurred to him that perhaps he was running away instead of running toward his dreams. A little tug grew in his heart to go back to Lily, but he pushed it aside. He closed the door to his heart to make the tug go away.

He closed his eyes to hide from the pain in his heart just before he felt a strong bump. He quickly opened his eyes and looked around. The light was fading fast and the twilight made it hard to see more than ten feet around him on the deck. He ran to the starboard side, grabbed the rail and looked forward toward the bow. A darkened craft had pulled alongside the steamboat and he could see men jumping the rails.

He grabbed the first thing he could, a grappling hook on a long pole and swung it toward the men that were quickly moving toward him in the darkness. The hook struck one in the head and Evan heard a thump as the invader hit the wood deck.

An arm shot around his neck from behind and caught him in a headlock. "Just tell us where Evan McEwen is and we'll be on our way."

Evan heaved forward and the man flipped over Evan's back and onto the ground in front of him. Evan took a wide stance looking for others.

The man on the floor groaned.

"You found him. Now tell me what your business is with me!" Evan asked.

In the shadows, a blast of light sparked. A gunshot rang out. Before he could react, white hot fire pierced his right shoulder knocking him backwards. His left hand went to his shoulder as he lost his balance. His shirt was warm and wet. He landed with a thud, his head hitting the edge of a supply box beneath the rail next to the turning paddles. The paddles sprayed his face with cold water. He couldn't open his eyes and nausea overtook him. The hiss of falling water blocked all sound. Consciousness evaded him, pushing him in a deep hole in his mind. The pain in his shoulder and head receded until he felt nothing at all.

***

Lily stood in front of the class watching the students work. The advanced male students were writing a summary

126

of the bible verses about the walls of Jericho falling. The novice males and all the female students were copying the verse onto their slate.

The girls were coming along learning to write. Despite Brian's assumption that the girls could not be taught to write, especially the poor girls, they were eager and able to make letters. Of course, Lily knew they would be. Girls now were no different than girls a hundred years from now.

The boys had raised their eyebrows when she'd given the assignment. One boy even raised his hand to protest. He told her that if girls learned to write, what would boys do? She understood his fear. Change is always hard when you can't see what the outcome will be, but she knew the outcome. Men were still just as needed in a world where women could read and write.

She walked down the rows of desks looking over their progress. She felt confident she was still holding to the curriculum the town council required. The children were still learning about the Bible.

The door in the back of the room opened wide and Brian Everbright stood silhouetted with sunlight. He looked like an angel straight from heaven. He closed the door behind him and walked slowly toward her, looking at the children's work as he went. His right eyebrow shot up as he passed a girl about ten years old making letters.

Lily sucked in a breath. He looked up at her and pursed his lips. His pace quickened and when he got to her, he held her by the arm and escorted her to the front the room.

"Can you explain to me what you are doing here?" he asked under his breath.

His pale blue eyes made her want to melt into her shoes. The fight for her wits overcame her bodily reaction to being so close to him, "Certainly, Mr. Everbright," she straightened, "the children are studying the Bible using a variety of academic methods." She lifted her chin an almost imperceptible degree defying him to challenge her.

"Miss Wallingsford, you know very well it's not the subject matter that I'm inquiring about. More specifically, and to the point, why are girls wasting school time with writing?"

She pulled her arm free from his hand and stood squarely in front of him. "Sir, copying lines is a proven technique for memorization. You require them to memorize bible verses and my method accomplishes this end. I take exception to your questioning my methods if it accomplishes the learning target."

He exhaled and looked down before resuming his searching gaze, "You are going beyond what is required."

"And when has going above and beyond in one's endeavors been frowned upon?"

"When it causes trouble."

Her eyes widened as her mind reeled, "Trouble? Sir! My job is to educate. If an educated populace creates trouble, I would ask for whom it's troubling and have them examine what they gain from having this group remain subordinate. What power are they protecting that is only gained by subjugating through ignorance?"

He ground his teeth and clenched his fists. "Might I remind you," he struggled to whisper, "you are here as a substitute. You should not flatter yourself to think you will remake our curriculum. You have a lot to lose if you persist." Having had the last word, he turned and strode out of the room.

She stood next to her desk stunned. She gripped the edge to keep from losing her balance as her eyes drifted across the students' heads. They were all still busily working on

128

their tasks, except Priscilla. Priscilla watched her with sad eyes. As though she knew this couldn't continue. Hope seemed to evaporate around her.

Red fury rose in Lily's chest. She would not be deterred. Priscilla had no way to fight for her right to learn. It was up to Lily to stand up for her. Not realizing it, she had moved to Priscilla's desk. She knelt down beside her.

"Priscilla, how are doing with your letters? Let me see." She picked up the slate and examined the scrawled attempts.

Priscilla bowed her head.

"My dear girl, you are doing so well! I want you to keep working and soon you will be as pleased with your progress as I am." She smiled broadly at the girl. Light danced in Priscilla's eyes.

"You think so, ma'am?" her timid defeated voice had an upturn at the end showing she wanted to believe her.

"Oh, I am certain. I can tell you have a willingness to learn which, I believe, is the key to success."

Priscilla beamed before diving back into her work with her tongue sticking out the corner of her mouth.

Lily stood up and took a deep breath. Brian's effect on her was unmistakable. A surge of rebelliousness welled up in her. She wanted the girls to learn to write, no doubt, but she also had the urge to do exactly the opposite of what Brian wanted her to. It was a dangerous combination because he did not seem like the kind of Victorian man that would tolerate a wife with her own mind, even if that was the very thing that attracted him to her.

She leaned against the desk again and stared absently out the tall plate glass windows. The bright blue sky seemed to stretch all the way to outer space. A day dream scene began to play out in her mind. She and Brian were married and he had told her not to do something. She had gone behind his back and done it anyway and he was furious. She felt bad for what she had done, but in her heart of hearts, she wanted to do what she'd done. She was not going to be pushed around and lorded over.

That wasn't quite it, though. She wanted him to lose his mind. She wanted him to unleash his fury on her. She wanted to feel the tidal wave of passion he would let loose. The secure feeling of being owned pulled at the fringes of her emotions. The price was high, but the security of his attention made it seem worthwhile. She longed to belong and who better to belong to than a man who could give her everything?

The clearing of a young man's throat pulled her out of her fantasy. He was finished and ready to be evaluated. She shoved her thoughts in a closet of her mind and returned to the bright light of day.

***

Evan grimaced as the red-hot pain of the wound reminded him to be still. Dull aching throbbed in his chest. He let out a low groan and tried to feel his torso. Soft fingers held his hand back.

"Lily?" he whispered.

"Sorry, honey. There's no Lily here." The feminine voice rang through the air like a melody of chimes.

"Where am I?" he asked while trying to open his eyes to the painful bright light of day.

"Mound City, Illinois. You were in a river boat accident, but your injury is actually a gunshot wound. You were found floating on a piece of the deck."

He tried to focus on the ceiling, but the room was turning on a lopsided horizon making him nauseous. "I remember shots ringing out, a blast from a rifle lightin' up the deck.

But," he struggled to hold the memory, "I dinnae remember anything after that. Just a crack on the back of my head when I fell back."

His vision settled and he could see a fuzzy outline of a woman in a white coat. Her hair was pulled up in a loose bun. Her lacy high black collar stood around her neck over her coat. She examined him with the unaffected observation.

"Yes, you have a contusion at the base of your skull that will be sore for a while. You needed surgery to remove the bullet from your chest. It did pierce your lung, so you may be coughing up some blood for a few days, but all in all, you should be alright."

"So why was I float'n on a piece of the deck?"

"The Granite State sternwheeler sank when it struck the rocks downriver from Grand Chain. Apparently, it was commandeered by bandits who inadvertently ran it aground when Captain Marr refused to assist them."

"Good man! Did he survive?"

"Yes, yes he did. He was able to give a full report."

Evan relaxed but something about the sternwheeler kept eating him. His right arm was in a fabric sling that held his pectoral muscles still. White strips of fabric were wrapped around his chest, but his muscular shoulders and the left side of his torso was exposed. Feeling naked in front of a woman, he glanced at her face to see if she was looking at him. She had begun to take notes in a book and appeared disinterested in his physique. He turned his head annoyed with his current status, stuck in a hospital.

Turing back to her quickly, "Who are ye?" He realized he didn't know who she was.

"I'm Doctor Emeline Cooke. This is my infirmary. Do you take issue with being treated by a woman?"

"Not at all. I'm still alive so ye must be good at what ye do."

She chuckled dryly, "You were very lucky you didn't drown."

The dizziness took hold again and he winced.

"You need to sleep. That was a good blow to the head. Get some rest and we can talk more tomorrow."

"On the sternwheeler, the gunmen, they knew my name." The room started spinning.

If she said anything after that, he didn't hear. The pounding in his head took all his attention. In a blessed pull from consciousness, he lost himself in the darkness that took over his mind.

***

The boys filed out of the classroom quietly in two lines. The girls had left earlier that afternoon. The last one closed the doors behind him. Lily was pleased with the day's progress and smiled to herself. She turned and pulled her cloak off the hall tree in the corner. She lifted it around her shoulders and tied the black ribbon around her neck and picked up her lunch bucket.

The door slammed and she jumped. Expecting to see a student that had forgotten something, her brows arched when she saw Brian standing at the back of the classroom with his arms crossed.

"Oh! It's you."

"Miss Wallingsford, we need to discuss your teaching methods."

Setting her lunch bucket back on the shelf, "Certainly. I'm always ready for a discussion on how to improve education."

"Come and sit down." He extended his arm indicating the desk beside him.

She walked the length of the room and looked at the small desk and chair. He hadn't moved, so she realized he was planning to stand. All the body language strategies to exert power were in his favor. She hesitated before sitting in the desk that was too small for her legs.

He moved to stand in front of her still crossing his arms. At first he said nothing and just stared at her with laser blue eyes. "I speak with all the authority of the town council. You knew what was expected of you. You have chosen to disobey our instructions."

She didn't like the tone of this. Suddenly it seemed too much like a father chastising a small child. "Excuse me," she interjected.

His hand shot up with his palm facing her, "You will not interrupt."

A rush of adrenaline pulsed through her veins until a dull throb washed over her fingertips and toes. The split-second of shock was replaced with anger.

How dare he speak to me with so little respect?

"We will not tolerate insubordination in your position. I'm sure you are aware of the integrity guidelines for a teacher."

Following him down this rabbit hole of surprises, she felt a creeping fear of what he was going to do next. "What," she choked on the word, "What are you going to do? Are you firing me?"

A pained smile turned up the corners of his mouth. "You're interrupting again, but I will answer your question since this is the first time. No, silly girl. We need a good teacher. You just need some guidance, and," he paused, "discipline."

133

Her breath caught in her chest. She froze with wide eyes. "Please stand and hold on to the back of the chair."

She couldn't move. The horrifying realization that the man intended to spank her turned her blood to ice.

He spoke again, this time more forcefully, "Get up and put your hands on the back of the chair."

Victorian age or not, she was not about to let this play out as he intended, "MISTER Everbright! You will not lay a hand or any other object on me without my consent! Is that clear?"

She didn't wait for him to answer, but his eyes shot open as big as saucers as she continued, "If you would like to review my lesson plans or observe my teaching methods, I would be more than happy to oblige you. I am quite accustomed to supervisors with more responsibility than you looking over my shoulder and nit-picking my every word. That's part of being a professional educator. Now let's talk about your professionalism. Am I to understand you have an archaic notion that corporal punishment should be used on grown women, let alone children?"

"Go ahead and say your piece, Miss Wallingford. Get it all out."

"I see you aren't used to working with a college-educated, professional adult. I will overlook your lack of insight in this area this time, but if you ever," she took a step forward and pointed her finger at his nose and repeated, "if you EVER, make a mistake like that again, you can find yourself a new teacher for this school!"

She turned and picked up her lunchbox, when he held her by her arm. She looked down at his hand before looking him in the eye. "Miss Wallingsford," his words were nearly a hiss in his clenched teeth. He pinched the bridge of his nose and took a deep breath before speaking again. "Now I am going to explain something to you. It's crucial you understand. From the moment I first saw you on Main Street I knew I wanted you. We can continue with proper courting, but understand, I get what I want. From what I can see you have little to nothing to offer a man of my stature with regard to wealth. I have taken the liberty of checking out your story and I have found no mother and father in Frankfort."

She gasped and stared at him.

"I'm not sure what game you are playing with the Blacks, but frankly, I don't care. All I hope is that you can see the value of having caught my eye and what that can mean for you. Just as important, I hope you can see the destruction I can cause for you if I want to." He gave her a pitying smirk.

"What are you talking about?"

"Ah. I will have to spell it out for you." He continued to look down his nose at her. "The spread of the story that you come with no ties to decent society. A petty rumor of indiscretion with me, of how you had the nerve to ask me for money afterward-- It wouldn't take much and you would be run out of town on a rail. My word in this town carries far more weight than a fly-by-night waif that showed up half-dressed on a creek bank."

"But why? Why would you do that? What have I done to you?"

He chuckled and then took her hands firmly in a mock posture of deference. "My darling, I don't want to do anything like that. Quite the contrary. I don't care where you came from. A meddling family of in-laws would complicate my life anyway. What I want is to dress you in the finest silk, have your hair coiffed like a queen, and have you hanging on my arm. I want to bed you for my pleasure every night. You are like a beautiful bird that I can't take my eyes off."

"You want to own me like a pet?"

"And is that bad? I want to pamper you. I want to adore you. I want all the world to envy me because you are mine. You would be the envy of every woman."

Creases made dark lines in the porcelain skin of her forehead.

"Come, come, Lily. What I offer you is an easy choice. You would have the life of a precious bird of paradise. If it would please my wife to teach, then I will allow it. However, remember your place. All of this good fortune comes from my hand."

She shifted and looked up at him with wide eyes.

"Just the same, I don't take well to not getting what I want. Therefore, if you disobey my directive for the curriculum, or if you try to derail my plans to marry you, there will be consequences for you," he paused as a thought gathered in his head, "and the Blacks."

"You would hurt William and Bettie?"

"Hurt is a strong word. Let's just say I can make life in Stephensport difficult for them."

"When Evan finds out about your threats, he won't let you harm them." She shook her head in frustration and started to bolt away. He caught her by the wrist.

"Lily, it's your choice, of course. I wouldn't count on Mr. McEwen if I were you. I'm sure he is long gone. His type isn't dependable."

"You don't know Evan." She hissed.

"Time will tell. You do have the zest of a wild filly and that thrills me to no end." He pulled her against him, wrapping her in his arms.

Locked in his hold, she couldn't move. His mouth covered hers in a crushing kiss as though he meant to tame a thunderstorm. For a brief moment, the closeness of him made her dizzy. How could someone so controlling, make her want to melt into him. His searching tongue pressed into the inner sanctum of her mouth, demanding her submission. It was so easy to let her thinking brain lose consciousness, to let go and let him take what he wanted. The burning lava in her pelvis heated until an ache grew. Her body betrayed her again. As much as she hated him, she wanted him. She wanted to be his and she hated herself for it.

Her brain jerked awake in ratcheting thoughts of alarm, "Nnnnn," she hummed, "Nnnnn, no." He encircled her tighter like a python, pressing his kiss deeper.

Without releasing her mouth, he said, "You belong to me, Lily. You can't fight it. I feel the heat of your core calling to me."

She pushed against him to get away.

"Go then, for now," he dropped his arms, "but don't think of denying me."

She ran and left the door ajar as she flew down the stone steps. Her heart pounded in her chest and the scenery was going past at sixty miles per hour. She couldn't focus on anything but getting home.

She rounded the drive that ended at Black's Farm and a rush of relief washed over her. Home. She darted behind a tree, as though she were being pursued and the tears came. Leaning on her left forearm against the tree, she let loose of the racking sobs. All the fear and shock of her encounter with Brian bubbled up. Closing her eyes and gritting her teeth, she wept. Brian was everything she would never want in a mate. His controlling overbearing, entitled attitude made her scream. At the same time, his confidence, assertiveness, and drive was so seductive. The conflicting reactions in her made her head hurt.

Startled, she jumped at the feel of a small fingers touching her right hand. "Ack!"

"Don't be frightened, Miss Wallingsford. It's just me, Carlton."

She knelt down and smiled, relieved. She dashed the tears from her cheeks. Her heart was in her throat. Carlton was the picture of childlike innocence with big blue eyes. She tousled his golden honey hair.

"What's the matter, ma'am?"

She sucked in a breath and then pushed down the anxiety, "Oh! I'm fine. Just a hard day."

"Oh, yes. I have hard days, too. Sometimes I bawl just like you were." He smiled at her.

"Sweet Carlton. You are such a dear boy."

His cheeks pinked. "Thank you, ma'am. You want some lemonade? Momma made some just now."

"Yes. I'd like that."

They walked together to the house. She was so glad to have the company of this sweet boy, but her mind kept replaying the scene at the schoolhouse.

After dinner, William retired to his study and she sat with Bettie in the parlor.

"Bettie, have, has—" she stammered. Bettie waited for her to find the words. "What I mean is, in your experience, is it common for men to, to beat or discipline women?" Her face turned as red as a tomato and she could feel the heat rise off her cheeks.

Bettie studied her a minute before answering, "Generally, no. Not that I know of directly. That's not to say it doesn't happen. Of course, dear William would die a thousand deaths before he'd lift a hand to me. And of course, I'd throttle him if he tried. That works out well that way." She chuckled.

138

Bettie continued, "But there are men that consider women their property and feel they can do whatever they want. The old 'rule of thumb', you know?"

"I had heard of that, but didn't think, well, I thought that was back in the Middle Ages."

"Oh, darlin'! For all the finery and talk of enlightenment, I can assure you, behind closed doors, it is still very much the Middle Ages. You'll never prove it, but if you watch, you see the signs. Women who don't come out in public for a week or so. Chances are they are nursing bruises. We have very little rights. That's why you have to be very careful who you marry. Even then, men hide their ways until it's too late. That Brian Everbright seems nice, doesn't he?" Her voice floated with a pregnant pause as though she suspected trouble.

Lily's eyes shot up like a laser. "I can't say."

"Think long and hard, Lily. A man like him can change everything."

A tear slipped from the corner of Lily's eye.

"Now, there, honeycakes." Bettie scooted toward her and pulled out a white handkerchief with pink embroidery around the edge. She handed it to Lily.

"This is too pretty to wipe my face with!" said Lily.

Bettie let out a belly laugh, "Honeycakes, you are too pretty for that handkerchief. It's the one that should be worried."

They both laughed and Bettie put her arm around Lily's shoulders and squeezed. "At least you don't have to choose between him and Mr. McEwen anymore."

"But how would I know what's best?"

Bettie smiled at her. "No man is perfect or they would be Jesus, himself. So, get that notion out of your head first.

Secondly, know what is most important to you. Lastly, find the man who shares that sentiment and forgive him the rest."

"It seems so easy when you say it like that."

"Oh, honey! That last bit about forgiving him the rest is the hardest part. It's a cost for getting what's truly important. Sometimes, a high cost. And then some women will expect him to change the imperfect part, even though they got their most important desire. That's unfair to him and a fool's errand for you."

***

Light flashing in his eyes pushed away the blessed sleep. He felt cold fingers on his cheekbone and eyebrow. His eyes fluttered open as he tried to turn his head to the side. "Stop that!"

"Whoa! Nelly! I'm just seeing if you are sleeping or in a coma! You weren't waking up."

"I'm in no coma! Stop blinding me!"

Dr. Cooke sighed and straightened. She stood beside the bed. "I'm glad to see you are conscious."

"How long have I been out?"

"It's been several hours since we last talked. You lost a great deal of blood before you got to me and then during your sleep, you got restless and tore your stitches open. I actually stitched you closed again and you never woke up. I was beginning to get worried about you."

"I see." He glanced at the window. The black sky was dotted with sparkling stars. The oil lamp glowed on the small chest of drawers behind her. "It's late, isn't it?"

"It is. My husband and I are staying here at the clinic tonight so I can be close by."

"Yer husband? You're married?"

She smiled. "Yes. Does that surprise you?"

140

"I just- I mean, aye. How do you have time to be a doctor?"

She chuckled and shook her head. "We all get twenty-four hours a day."

"I mean, how do you manage a home and family with yer work?"

"Very well, thanks. My work affords me an income to hire others to do wash and cook meals. As for children, well, God has not blessed me with them."

He studied her as she waited for his response to her answer. She was a remarkably handsome woman. He wondered if she was a pampered wife of a wealthy man that let her play at what she wanted. "What does yer husband do?"

"My husband has a lumber mill here in town." She didn't appear affected at all by his questions as though she was accustomed to such a response. "Does that surprise you?"

"A bit. It is unusual."

"Go ahead and ask your next question. I know it's there."

His eyebrow pressed down at her request. The question was there. He just couldn't in good conscious bring himself to ask it.

She sighed, "You are wondering how my husband feels about my career."

Both brows shot up this time.

"He is very proud of me, as I am of him."

Evan smiled. It made such sense. Of course her husband would be proud. Why was that hard to imagine? He had known women who were healers or teachers or seamstresses, but they all quit their career when they married. Now that he thought about it, it wasn't fair for them to feel like they had to do that. "He is a good man."

"I am quite lucky. I know that."

"Were ye finished with medical school when ye met him?"

"No. We have known each other since we were children. He always knew my dream was to be a doctor. He asked me to marry him when I was sixteen but said he would wait until my education was finished. When I graduated and finished my internship, I came back and opened my infirmary. Then we were married. There was never a question about my career."

"Do you think it would have been different if you had met your husband after you finished school?"

She thought for a minute and then said, "No. I would never sacrifice my dreams to please another. If I had met him afterward, either he would have to love me with my dreams or he would not have truly loved me."

Evan nodded. "The way ye put it, it makes perfect sense."

"How could it not make sense? Loving another means letting them be who they are."

"I suppose you're right." He smiled.

"You know, I don't even know your name?"

"Evan McEwen."

"So what was your business on the Granite State?"

He looked away before answering, "Traveling."

"I see. Traveling to something or away from something?"

He looked back and searched her eyes.

"I see a great deal in this river city. I've found there are three kinds of men. One works on the paddle wheelers. One is running from something and the last is searching for something. Captain Marr told me you were not one of his regular men, so you have to be one of the last two possibilities."

He smirked at her, amused at her ability to deduce his story. "Maybe a little of both."

She smiled. "Where is your heart? Did you leave it behind or is it downriver?"

"I can see why yer a good doctor. Ye have a way of getting to the root of a problem."

"I believe a doctor should treat the whole person, not just the body."

"My heart," he paused, "is firmly planted in my chest and not staying anywhere it's not wanted."

"Ah. There we go. She turned you down?"

He pursed his lips and closed his eyes. "I'm a realist, ma'am."

She tilted her head studying him. "So, you didn't wait around to see if she chose you or another. That's not a realist. It's someone who's afraid."

His chest swelled as his eyes widened. "Afraid? No, ma'am. I'm not afraid."

"You gave up your life there to avoid being the one empty handed *if* she chose another. That sounds like fear to me."

"You're wrong! All due respect, ma'am, but-"

She interrupted, "What if she loves you?"

He stared at her in silent shock.

"That is what you need to be afraid of." She got up and started to leave. Before closing the door behind her, she said, "I'll check on you in the morning."

***

Lily couldn't sleep. Her fury had calmed to where the only thing running through her was his words: *You will cease teaching the girls to write. It is absolutely forbidden.*

His threats seemed ludicrous. What burned her up the most was not that girls of this time were forbidden to learn to write, but rather that only privileged girls were taught.

Girls from wealthy families were sent to private schools and educated to be quite literate. This decision by Brian and the rest of the town council was meant just for the poor and middle-class girls. It was forcing a class of women to stay down. She couldn't understand what difference it made as long as the boys still got all the attention they deserved. Why couldn't she teach the girls?

The only obvious answer was that Brian and those like him wanted to make sure they stayed at the top of the heap. They were pulling up the gang plank. It ensured there was a lower class to raise them up in society. After all, if just anyone could make it, then what pride could a privileged class have for merely existing?

Evan's face came to mind. She could see him working his brother's estate, never able to move ahead. He would never be the laird unless by some tragedy. No matter how hard he worked, his place was set.

"But isn't that why America is different? And if we are different, why are they trying to hold these girls back just to keep themselves ahead?"

She imagined Evan stepping off a ship in America and having the hope of making a life that was built with his own hands. All the hope of possibilities was there in his eyes. Something tickled her mind. That look was familiar. Then she saw her girls in her mind. They were sitting around her in the classroom listening to her as she told them she would teach them to write. They knew. Education meant everything. They may never be wealthy, but being literate would give them power over their own life.

She wondered where Evan was. Out the window, she saw the stars twinkling against the black void of space. Somewhere under God's heaven, Evan was out there. A longing grew in the pit of her stomach. She imagined him lying in a bed shirtless with his hand behind his head. A nervous thrill struck her like lightening as she imagined his chiseled torso. Muscles, well-trained from steadying a plow or wielding an ax, formed a shadowed undulation of flesh.

With all the force of a real slap, reality struck her that he was gone. Her ambivalence had let him slip through her fingers. She had chased a life of comfort and found only shadows. A life with Brian would be a nightmare. A tear welled in the corner of her eye and finally rolled down her cheek.

"Oh, grandma! It's no better here than in my own time."

***

Evan dreamed of Lily all night. He searched for her in the woods. He would get close to her and she would evaporate. He could hear her giggle at him and he felt like a fool. Then he would see her in a clearing in Brian's arms. Brian would laugh at him and squeeze Lily tighter while groping her backside. He would try to run to her and she would tell him to stay away.

He was relieved to wake up when the doctor opened the door carrying his breakfast tray.

"Good morning, Mr. McEwen. Here's a good breakfast. How do you feel?"

"Well enough, it seems." He pushed himself up in bed with one arm causing the sheet to fall around his waist. His flexed left bicep gave the impression he was healthy as an ox. The sling holding his right arm still was the only giveaway that this man was not Hercules himself. Locks of dark wavy hair covered the side of his face as he looked down and realized he was half naked. He pulled the sheet back up to cover his chest.

She put the tray with short legs down over his lap. I think you are doing well enough to go soon. Let me check your wounds."

"Certainly, ma'am. I thank ye, kindly."

The doctor undid the knot at the back of his neck releasing the sling. He winced as his arm straightened. "Yes. You'll be sore for a bit. Those muscles pull on your wound." She then began to unwind the strip of cloth that wrapped around his chest and back. When she got it halfway unwrapped, she was able to see the square of white cotton over the wound and pealed back the corner to take a peak. "It's healing well. No infection. A fine job, if I say so myself. Keep it covered and clean." She rewound the strip of fabric around him and tucked it in. Then she gently lifted the ends of the sling fabric and retied it behind his neck.

"I see no reason not to release you this morning."

"That's good. I can be on my way."

"And where is that, Mr. McEwen?"

"Farther down river, I suppose."

She made tisk tisk noises.

"You don't approve?"

"No, sir."

"And why is that?"

"Just a hunch I have. I know what half a man looks like when I see him."

"Half a man?" he grimaced.

"I can treat your body, but your heart is still torn. You thrashed in your bed all night searching for her. Go back, Mr. McEwen."

He sighed. He knew she was right. Something felt wrong. He had to go back.

Some hours later he was standing on the dock waiting for a paddle wheeler to tie off and open its decks. His left arm

146

was in a sling to protect the muscles that were healing in his chest. His brown overcoat was slung around his left shoulder over his arm. A man in a captain's hat stepped off onto the deck.

"Sir!" Evan stepped forward to get his attention. "I was wondering if ye might have some work aboard that I could do to earn passage to Stephensport, Kentucky."

The captain looked at his arm and then back at Evan's face. "What could a one-armed man actually do on a boat?"

Evan was stumped himself and paused. "I, I," he stammered.

"Sorry, buddy. I can't help you."

As the captain was about to turn away, Evan blurted, "I can clean. I mean, I can wipe down tables and walls. I can polish brass fittings."

The captain studied him for a minute and then said, "All right. Get started. Ask for Danny in the kitchen and tell him to find you some polish and a rag."

Evan smiled and tipped an imaginary hat. The captain sauntered off and Evan stepped aboard.

After the crew shared a midday meal, the paddle wheeler pulled away from the dock and floated freely on the brown churning river. Evan worked on brass lanterns and fittings on the bow, rubbing the polish in to reveal a yellow shine. Going upriver was slower than coming downriver. The two-story behemoth slowly splashed against the white caps.

This paddle wheeler carried passengers as well as a small amount of cargo. Staterooms lined the port and starboard decks on the first floor. The second floor housed the dining room and observation deck. White wrought iron railings lined the edge of the open-air observation deck above him. He was taking in the details of this river belle when he looked up to find a lady watching him from above. When

147

she saw him look her way, she turned away as a proper lady would. Her blue and white gown glowed in the afternoon sun. Her white parasol fluttered in the gentle breeze.

Evan was painfully aware of his status as the working class. In Scotland, he garnered some respect as the laird's brother. In America, though, there was no caste system. Right of birth made no difference unless the family you were born into happened to be wealthy. That same family could be thrust into the lower class if they lost their wealth.

Evan turned back to his work and did it with earnest. One day, he would have the respect he craved and it would be earned. He would have it by the work of his own hands. He realized now that running from pain wasn't going to get him anywhere. Whatever life Lily chose for herself was not his to brood over. If it wasn't with him, then so be it. He would stay steadfast to his dreams. The Blacks had been good to him. They gave him work and a place to live while he worked for them. He had opened an account with the bank and made steady deposits. He'd planned to have the account transferred to wherever he landed on the Mississippi. By his estimates, he would be able to buy some farmland within a year. Not much, but enough to get started.

***

Two days passed without any sign of Brian. Lily had gone over their conversation in her head numerous times. For a multitude of reasons, she should allow Brian to continue with his plans. Even Bettie pushed her to consider him. If she didn't, the consequences would be dire. She wasn't sure what he would do to the Blacks but she had no doubt he could ruin them.

148

She sat in the parlor gazing out the side window while Bettie worked on a piece of embroidery when a knock at the door jolted her out of her reverie.

"Would you get that, dear? I'm knee deep in my work."

"Certainly." She said as she rose and crossed the room. As she reached to grasp the door handle, a flood of hesitation passed through her. Hesitation and dread. She knew it was him. He had come for an answer. She pulled the door open to the sight of him standing with his hand on his hip. He wore a black informal suit and a dark hat with rounded brims. His eyes caught hers like a maestro.

With every expectation that she would give herself to him, he said, "Darling Lily. Just whom I came to see."

"Mr. Everbright. Won't you come in?" She stepped to the side to let him in while her face gave away nothing of what she felt. If he could have owned her mind, too, he would have seen the war inside her. There was no doubt chemistry was there. Her body immediately ached to touch him. Her mind numbingly gave in to his demand for ownership. But, her heart railed against the bars of its cage. Her mind spoke up and told her that two out of three was pretty good.

Brian stepped across the threshold and waited for her to close the door. Bettie swung into action and stowed her sewing in the basket at her feet.

"Mr. Everbright! To what do we owe the pleasure? Perhaps you couldn't stay away from our dear Lily?" Bettie winked at Lily. Lily wanted to shoot her.

"Actually, you are quite right." He smiled at Lily. A jolt of electricity shot through her core.

"Please come in and have a seat. I'll call for William to join us." Bettie turned and darted down the center hallway.

"After you, my darling." He motioned for her to go into the parlor. She kept her face stoic and sat on the sofa.

He sat beside her and took her hand. She let him. She was so torn, she could only comply. He leaned in and kissed the ridge of her ear.

Oh, I wish he wouldn't do that. Her arms went limp and she would have collapsed if she wasn't sitting.

He whispered against her ear, "My Lily, my tender cabbage, I want you."

Her gut clenched in a visceral reaction to his bold claim using the possessive words. She was just about to make a comment about being called a 'tender cabbage' when William came around the corner.

"Mr. Everbright! What a pleasant surprise." William stepped into the foyer.

Brian casually straightened and then stood to shake William's hand.

"Please, sit down. Can I get you a drink?"

"Very kind of you, but no. I came to discuss a matter with you." He turned and winked at Lily.

"I see. Please," William motioned to the sofa, "let's sit and hear what you want to talk about."

Brian resumed his seat next to Lily while William sat in the wing chair across from them. Bettie moved behind William's chair and rested her arm on the back.

"I understand it hasn't been long, but I find myself taken with Lily. I would like to ask your permission, as the only male relative of hers in the area, to court Lily with the intention to marry her."

William stood up and put his hands on his hips thinking. "Well, this is sudden. I surely don't feel it's my place to speak for her father."

Bettie came around the chair, "Dearest William, surely her father would not object to Mr. Everbright. We could send a post out first thing in the morning with the news."

Lily sat there like stone. She felt paralyzed. She'd dreamed of this moment for most of her life: The moment when a man would pledge to marry her. Here he was. She turned her head slowly and looked at him, trying not to betray the jangled thudding of her heart to anyone.

The most eligible man in Stephensport, a wealthy man of means, crazy good looking, and here he was asking for permission to marry her. She should have been breathless, panting with delight, but she wasn't. An emotion poked at her but she couldn't name it. It wasn't ambivalence because of Evan. It wasn't revulsion for his opinion of women. It wasn't even fear of his threat.

Her mouth closed from her slack jaw expression and she pursed her lips. She unconsciously leaned away slowly. Her cheeks flushed and she tipped her chin up defiantly. She may not have been able to control her body's reaction to his touch but she surely could control her own life.

How dare he? He didn't wait for her answer to his diabolical proposition. "William, I insist that my father reply to Mr. Everbright. It is his prerogative."

Brian turned to her and she could see the sparks in his eyes. She had effectively shut down the proposal, at least for now.

"Oh, yes," William seemed relieved, "I'll wire Frankfort first thing tomorrow."

"You do that, Mr. Black. You do that. I look forward to hearing what you find out." Brian didn't take his eyes off Lily as he spoke to William.

"Lily," Bettie said, "let's go in the kitchen and make some tea." The ladies silently exited the room.

***

151

Evan stepped off the dock and was at once both happy and pained to be back in Stephensport. It was late in the day and few people were about on Main Street. The thought of coming back to Black's Farm with his tail between his legs made him nauseous. There was no other option. He could take a room at the inn. Besides, when the Black's found out he was in town, they would want answers. They would want to know what they had done to earn his aloofness. All that aside, the last thing he wanted to do was to get in Lily's way if she didn't want him.

"Mr. McEwen!" A small boy called out from across the road. He waved his arm wildly.

"Young Master Smith! How is it with you?" he answered.

The boy ran toward him. Breathlessly, "There's a wire for you. You need to go to the telegraph office."

"Aye? Certainly, then. I'll go now."

Evan briskly walked the boardwalk in front of the stores to reach the telegraph clerk in the post office. As he approached, he could see the light still on and took a deep relieved breath. He pushed the door open and the little bell tinkled announcing his arrival.

"Ah! Mr. McEwen. I wasn't sure how we would get your message to you since you'd left town. Good to see you." The clerk stood up and turned to the counter behind him. He thumbed through a box of small slips of paper and found the one he was looking for. He smiled as he held it out to Evan, "I trust this is good news for you."

Evan gave him a quizzical look and took the telegram. He read the telegram twice trying to understand. It was from his brother, the Laird. Due to an act of kindness toward the Crown, his family had been rewarded a substantial amount of gold. His brother wanted him to share in the windfall and had the bank of Scotland transfer the value of the gold to an account at the bank in Stephensport.

Evan stood stock still forgetting to breathe.

The telegraph clerk smiled bigger than before, "Good news for you, eh?"

"My God," Evan choked on the words! "I--, this is," he couldn't finish the sentence and tears streamed down his face.

The clerk reached out to shake his hand, "Now you can buy that farm you want, huh?"

"Praise be to God!" was all Evan could say. Rubbing his face to bring feeling back, he looked up at the clerk, "Thank you, good man. This message is a life changer."

The clerk nodded in acknowledgment and Evan darted out the door with the paper still in his hand. In a few long strides, he found himself in front of the bank and went inside. In the matter of a few minutes, he came back out a new man. He had money in his pocket and enough in an account to start the life he always wanted.

Now he had to decide if he was to return to Black's Farm or head to the inn. He decided he would stay at the inn since it was late. He would see William first thing in the morning, but tonight he would decide how it would be best to proceed. He had enough to buy farmland, but it would likely use up every bit of the money he now had. The farm would be his, but the life would be hard.

The other option would be to lease a home and work a trade. If Lily would have him, he would have a flush of cash to make a comfortable dwelling. He wished he could give Lily the charmed life Brian could offer her, but to do so would mean turning away from his dream of owning land and being a laird in his own right. He never resented his brother's birthright, but he did wish to have the same advantage. At least with his own farm, he would have something that would always be his. Even when he died, it would be there for his family. That was the legacy that burned in his heart.

***

The bright sun and crisp air invigorated him. Evan left the telegraph clerk's office after sending a message to his brother to let him know how much he appreciated him sharing the windfall. His brother didn't have to share it. He could have reinvested it into their land in Scotland. Having the support of his family so far from home strengthened him.

Walking along the boardwalk, he passed Ragdales' Drug Store and saw a sign in the window. The Louisville, St. Louis and Texas Railroad had unneeded land for sale. He stopped and studied the sign. The railroad had been given thousands of acres of land through a railroad land grant and was selling off unneeded land to raise revenue. Good, surveyed land was available in eighty-acre tracts in Stephensport. The sign said they offered ten-year credit options, but he could pay cash thanks to his brother.

Evan sucked in his breath. This was just what he needed. He turned his head toward the railroad depot and watched people milling around the station of the new railroad. A steam engine chugged alongside the station and let loose a billowing cloud of pent up steam into the air.

Evan's feet followed his head as the daydreams of his own farm filled his mind. In no time, he found himself at the door of the station. Stepping inside, the saw the ticket agent's window, the station manager's office, and a land agent's office. Three other men waited their turn to speak to the land agent.

154

He got behind them and craned his neck to hear what was being said inside. "Now, sir! That piece of land is prime land. I'll have to put it up for offers."

"But I was the first one here this morning!" said the farmer.

"I understand and I will duly note that. However, your bid is lower than the railroad thinks we can get for it." The land agent turned to the men in line, "I have an offer for a tract of eighty acres on the bank of Sinking Creek near the edge of town. If anyone would like to put a bid in, I'll hear it."

Evan stepped forward to look at the land agent's map. He felt the pull in his heart as though the land called him. He had to have this land. It was on the same creek as William's, just farther upstream.

"I raise his offer by five percent and I can pay cash on the money."

Not a sound was heard. All the men turned to Evan with wide eyes. Evan had not beheld such respect since he left his lands in Scotland. Acting on behalf of his brother in Scotland, he was given a wide berth, but here, he was looked upon as a common immigrant with nothing but the shirt on his back.

"Can anyone match his offer?" the land agent asked of the group. In an imperceptible movement, they all leaned back as an answer.

"Cash?" one of the men murmured. Common practice was a ten-year offer of credit to pay off the note. Evan didn't look like a high brow in a brown wool jacket and plain britches.

"Then it's sold to the man with the offer of cash. If you will excuse us, I have business to tend to with this gentleman."

155

The others filed out and left Evan to his business. Evan's chest swelled as he shook the land agent's hand when they were finished. Finally, he felt like the man he was born to be.

***

The sky was turning slate gray with a threat of snow when Evan turned his horse toward the house of Black's Farm. Lily saw movement outside by the front porch and stood to get a better look. She hoped it wasn't Brian. Her breath caught as she saw the hulk of a man on the chestnut stallion. He'd come back.

A zing of excitement split her core and she darted for the front door. She flung it wide and stood staring like a teenager. On his horse, he looked like he was fifteen feet tall. His brown suit gave away his station in life but she could swear she was staring at royalty. His respected Scottish lineage pulsed through his veins, to be sure. He sat straight in the saddle with the reins wrapped around his fist. His horse pranced, straining at the constraint. Evan's eyes caught hers and she knew she wanted nothing else but to love him and be loved by him. If this man loved her, she could conquer the world using the joy in her heart as fuel.

Without looking away, he gracefully dismounted. He looped the reins around a hitching post near the house. The horse settled and found a water trough at its feet. The air around her sizzled in the glow of her desire to be near him. He crossed the sleeping grass of winter and stood before her. Both searching each other's eyes for some sign of affirmation, they couldn't breech the emotional gap between them.

"It's been- so long- since I saw you," she muttered haltingly.

"I am sorry for leaving without saying goodbye."

"I worried about you." She noted the sling holding his arm under his coat.

He softened his posture and reached for her hand, "I have not stopped thinking of you the whole of the time."

A surge of joy flashed through her core when he touched her. "What brings you back now?"

"You." He pulled her closer to him holding her hands. "I want you for my wife if you will have me. I cannot live without you."

And with those simple, direct words, she knew she could never deny him. He didn't hide his love or want her for what she could do for him. It was the plea of a man-overboard calling for a ring buoy. Her heart would save him and he didn't even realize it was already his.

She leaned in and kissed him. At first he relaxed into it and let her tenderly give her response, melting in her answer that soothed his heart. Her hand went to his chest as he encircled her with his free arm, squeezing her against him. She felt his warm breath on her cheek like a soft caress, before exhilaration lit his eyes with passion. Leaning over her, he covered her mouth with his and plundered her lips. The heat from his body cut through their clothes from his chest to his thighs. She could have melted onto the ground if he didn't have her in such a firm grip.

Her head lolled back exposing the creamy white skin of her neck. He groaned and bit little bites from the nape of her neck to behind her ear.

"I love you, Lily," he whispered.

"I love you," she answered back.

"Tarnation!" came Bettie's voice. They both jumped back in surprise and Evan pulled on the bottom of his coat to straighten it out. "You'd both better come inside before there's talk all over town. Mr.McEwen, you have some explaining to do. Good to see you're alive and," she creased her brow upon seeing the sling. "Nearly well." She added the last part after she had already turned to go in, leaving the door wide open for them to follow. The screen door slammed behind her.

Evan looked with wide eyes of apology. She smiled at him and looped her arm in his. He relaxed and smiled back and they walked inside.

Bettie made herself comfortable in an occasional chair and picked up a tea pot and began to pour them each a cup. "I suppose we need to get caught up. It seems as though I have missed something."

Evan looked at Lily before speaking and then started, "I have come back to ask for Miss Lily's hand in marriage."

"Have you, now? You may need to get in line."

Evan shot Lily a pained look without even closing his mouth. "Are you spoken for, then?"

"No! No I am not. I have not accepted anyone else's offer of marriage."

"Now, Mr. Everbright might assume he already has an inroad," Bettie casually remarked.

Evan kept looking at Lily, who answered, "Mr. Everbright can think whatever he'd like, but I choose whom I shall marry. Besides, he is still waiting to hear from my father." Lily winked at Evan.

Bettie knew something was awry with Lily and this fact about her father did not escape her. "Yes, and do you think your father will respond," she paused, "soon?"

"It will be a while, I'm certain. My father is far away."

"I see." Bettie thought for a minute. "Perhaps we could assume Mr. McEwen has been to Frankfort while he was away and obtained a," she paused again, "a letter that could be presented to William?"

"Oh. Yes! A letter. That would do." Lily said looking at Evan.

Evan sighed. "It doesn't seem right, being underhanded."

"Given the circumstances, that's about all the permission you're going to get, I presume." Bettie said.

"Are you certain this is what you want?" he asked Lily. She nodded. "And Bettie, I must ask you to vouch for me that she is making a good choice. Ack! I have not told you my good fortune. My brother forwarded me a portion of the estate money from Scotland. I was able to purchase a parcel of land just upstream. I visited it today and it will make a fine homestead."

"Oh, Evan! How wonderful for you!" Bettie exclaimed.

"Really, Evan? Tell me about the land. What's it like?" Lily asked.

"It overlooks the curve of the river. You can see the steam over Stephensport from the paddlewheelers and the locomotives. There's good flat areas for farming and to build a house. There are also hills with trees and good areas to walk." He thought a minute. "It's a good place to make a family."

Heat rose to her cheeks. She could imagine nothing more wonderful than making a family with him and watching them grow.

"Well, then, I think any woman would be a fool to turn you away, especially if she loved you." Bettie looked at Lily. "And, I know it when I see it."

Evan and Lily looked at each and the smiles broke through the hesitation.

"Lily, would you accept my invitation to ride with me on my new homestead? I would like your opinion of it."

"Oh!" she stammered. A vision formed in her mind of her in a homespun dress churning butter as this man, straight out of a Highland romance novel, scoops her into his arms. She knew as well as anything that Evan would be a husband that would never tire of her and even better, would love her until the day he died. Here he was, willing to offer her his life, his name and his attention without hesitation. "Uh, yes. I would certainly love to see your new land. But we need to discuss--"

"Not now, darlin," Bettie interrupted. "You can figure out the little details later." She winked at Lily.

Lily saw a smile that broke loose across Evan's face. "Then I'll come by tomorrow morning and we will ride out together." He looked around at the dark gray sky. "It's going to be cold tonight. I hope you stay warm," he said with a twinkle in his eye. He leapt up on his stallion and tipped his hat toward her before setting off for the barn.

"You can breathe now, little lady." Bettie laughed at her.

Still dizzy, she looked at Bettie confused. Her mind caught up with her heart rate and she blushed. "That man will be the death of me."

"He will if you don't learn how to breathe around him!" ***

The morning frost covered the grass with glistening silver fuzz. On horseback, they followed the creek which gave off a ghostly mist rising up into the crisp morning air. Evan rode in front. His dark silky waves cascaded over the collar of his gray wool cloak. Lily wanted to run her fingers through it. She could feel the tickle of softness between her fingers just thinking about it. She closed her eyes and imagined laying on a blanket with him over her kissing her, her fingers running through his silky cool locks. Without

160

realizing it, she let go a quiet moan. Her horse stopped and jolted her out of her daydream.

"I hope I am the subject of your delightful daydreams." He smirked with self-satisfaction. They had stopped at a bend in the creek that opened to a wide flat meadow. The sunlight coming over the ridge caused the morning frost to glisten like a diamond farm. As she watched, the mist rose from the ground as though called back to the clouds from its evening getaway.

She forgot he was still watching her and clicked at the horse's sides to make it move ahead to get a better view.

"You like it then?" he asked.

She smiled, remembering he was there. "Is this your land? It's like heaven." She imagined how it would look in the summer with grass and trees so green it hurts your eyes, set against the backdrop of sapphire blue sky.

He moved his horse beside her, "It's our land, Lily. This is your home, too." He reached for her hand and she let him. He leaned across, pulling her hand toward him, and kissed her. Joy radiated from his broad smile. "Let me show you something! Follow me."

They galloped across the frosty meadow into the sunlight. The farther they went, the more the heat of the morning sun covered them, turning the frost into dew. The ground was waves of hibernating brown grass that clumped and crossed where it fell when the season changed. By the time they reached the other side, all the frost was gone and the dull faded color of winter had returned to the ground. The sun proudly reigned over them with white blasts of light surrounded by pale winter blue sky.

The forest of skeleton trees and occasional pine and cedar rose up like a wall beside the meadow. "Look back the way we came. See the puffs of white in the sky over there?"

161

He pointed back towards town. "That's Stephensport. That's steam from the sternwheelers and the train."

"Oh! Yes."

He got down off his horse and walked over to her. Reaching up he helped her slide off her horse. He wrapped his arms around her small waist and pulled her close to him. She could feel the heat of his skin through his clothes. As she looked into his eyes she couldn't imagine anything else mattering in the world. His head dipped and he kissed her tenderly. A quiet peace passed over her as she realized she had stopped breathing again.

"Evan, the sling. You're not wearing it. What happened to you, anyway?"

"A group of men tried to commandeer the river boat" He paused. "But, I remember just before I was shot, one knew my name."

"How would he know you? Were they from here?"

"I don't think so. I had never seen them before," he said.

"If you didn't know them, how would they know you?"

"I don't know, but I'm fairly sure they wanted to kill me."

"That makes no sense. Do you have any enemies?"

He laughed. "No. just that ox in the barn." He walked to a flat spot in the meadow. "Lily, what do you think about building our house here? On this spot?"

She nodded and smiled.

He pulled the blanket off the back of her horse with one hand, not letting go of her with the other. He shook out the blanket and tossed it on the ground and then sank to one knee. "On this ground, we will make our family. We will raise our bairns, laugh, love, dance, and live."

She sank down to her knees in front of him and kissed him softly.

"We will make a life and share the joy and the turmoil. Together. I give all of me to you."

"Are you sure, Evan? You know I am, uh, different. There may be things about me you will never understand."

He tossed his head back and laughed, "Oh woman, that you may come from another time would be the least confusing thing to understand about a woman!"

"Alright, then. I give you all of me, as well. I have to admit you take the notion of me being from the future pretty well."

"There are many things in this world I don't understand, but my mother always told me not to look a gift horse in the mouth."

"She sounds very practical." She looked up into his eyes. Lily felt the warm rush of desire coursing through her body and sank into the dizzy peace in her mind.

He lowered her to the ground and cradled her head under his arm. Pausing to survey the area around them, his face relaxed and the laugh lines around his eyes crushed against each other. With a broad smile of joy, he turned back to her catching sight of her soft pink lips. She couldn't take her eyes off him.

Referring back to her pledge, "And I accept you, all of you including your mysteries, as mine," he said.

The smile stretched farther across her face and her smooth cheek bones were even more prominent. A tender blush spread a warm glow when she realized he was going to kiss her. She wanted him now. She wanted to be his wife. She wanted his arms around her every night when she fell asleep and she wanted to see his face first thing every morning. More than that even, she wanted him to hold her next to him with nothing, not even clothes, to separate them. She wanted to feel the heat of his skin against her.

She imagined him slowly kissing his way from her neck to her belly button. A coursing flash of energy griped her from her chest to her thighs. She sucked in her breath and arched her back, pressing herself into him involuntarily. He responded instinctively and clamped down on her open mouth.

The insistent pressure of his kiss destroyed her resolve. A moan of sweet pleasure released in her distraction. She wrapped her arms around his waist as he let go of the passion he had held inside for so long. His kiss was deep and powerful. He claimed her as his future bride with this kiss. There was no misunderstanding. This was not just a marriage of convenience. He would love her with every fiber of his being.

Before long, they found themselves side by side looking up into the sky watching clouds pass by overhead.

"So, since we are daydreaming about our future, we need to talk about my plans for the school," she said.

"I agree. What are your plans, then?"

"I can't let the students down. The girls are depending on me to fight for them. The boys need more than rules and memorization. I'm not willing to give up my career."

He sighed. "I don't know how it will work,--"

"But—," she interrupted.

"Let me finish. I don't know how it will work, but I'm open to trying."

She thought about his words. It was quite a leap for a man of his time. The fact that he was open to trying with no strings, no lording, no conditions, was a giant step forward.

***

That evening, Lily sat with Bettie in the kitchen when they heard the knock at the door. Wide-eyed, she remembered the invitation to the ball with Brian.

Jumping up, "Oh, no! Bettie! I forgot!" Then she whispered, "Brian Everbright had invited me to a dinner ball with his parents. What am I going to do?"

"Oh, darlin! I don't know. Let me think." Bettie stood with her and took her hands.

"Whose carriage is that?" Evan strolled in the back door with a furrowed brow.

"Darling Bettie, Mr. Everbright is here. He says he is here to pick up Lily. What's this about?" William asked as he came through the hallway door.

The four of them stood looking from one to another until all eyes rested on Lily.

"I'll just have to tell him." She reached for Evan's hand.

"Well, this ought to be a spectacle to watch. We'll be right there with you, though, Lily."

Lily led the way and they all filed into the parlor.

Brian looked up from picking lint from his sleeve. "Ah there--, you aren't ready, then. Do you need time to dress?"

She stepped up to him and mustered all the courage she had. She knew he didn't like not getting his way. Her choices could very well have put William and Bettie in the line of fire, not to mention Evan.

"Mr. Everbright, I'm sorry I didn't send my regrets sooner, but I am otherwise engaged."

"What's this?" He looked down his nose at Evan. "I see you have returned. I suppose it's harder to drown a rat than one would expect." He looked at Evan with disdain. "Do you have something to do with this nonsense?"

"Yes," Lily answered. "Yes, he does. Apparently," she paused to gather strength. "Apparently, when Mr. McEwen

165

was out of town, he travelled to Frankfort and asked my father for my hand in marriage."

Brian straightened and looked down his nose even more so. His eyes narrowed in disbelief.

"He brought a hand-written letter and presented it to William. We are engaged to be married."

"It's the truth, Mr. Everbright," William said. "She speaks true."

Brian pursed his lips and jeered at Lily. "I see, Mr. Brown. "And tell me, how certain are you that it's written by her father's own hand, eh? How do we know he didn't have anyone write it for him? I'm not sure I would have taken that letter with such acceptance. He may have been miles away from Frankfort in the opposite direction."

"I am satisfied. I would trust Evan with my life."

"Is that so? Pardon me if I don't share your sentiment. I feel that something is awry. You know very well what my intentions are and yet you allow this, this hillbilly, to take what's promised to me? I'm not sure if I can stand by and allow such injustice."

Bettie and Lily shared a glance.

"There's nothing you can do about it, Mr. Everbright. What's done is done." Evan stepped in.

Brian turned to face him squarely. "Mr.McEwen, there is quite a bit I can do, in fact. First off, I may have evidence that shows there is no way you could have met with Lily's father. I could present that to a judge and sue for damages."

Evan didn't move or show any signs of weakness.

"However, what exactly would I gain from that? The work shirt off your back?" He turned then to William, "However, it seems the fault is shared by the man in whose custody she resides. To take a man's property is criminal and I will press charges."

Brian turned abruptly and strode out the door.

Lily let out a sigh. "That wasn't too bad."

"He's not finished." William said. "Brian Everbright is not a man to be slighted.

It had been a few weeks and she had not seen nor heard anything from Brian. She hoped he had moved on.

On a Monday morning, Lily found herself back in the classroom. Thoughts of Evan kept distracting her from the task at hand. She had the boys working on grammar while she sat with the girls in a circle on the floor. The morning light streamed in the window making a spotlight like a stage. A girl named Moira read from a primer. She read so slowly, sounding out every sound, that it was hard to follow the story. The other girls started looking around the room or out the window as they lost interest. Two girls whispered and giggled.

"Girls, let's read this paragraph together and then Moira can try again. Everyone together now." The group of eight girls read together. Some were louder than others and some skipped every other word. Lily chose one that read the best, "Mary, can you tell me what is happening?"

"Yes, ma'am. The girl is going to make bread and she is getting what she needs together."

"Good. Now Moira, try again to read it." Moira read it much faster now, only misreading a few words. "Good job, Moira."

"Alright, now." She took the hand of the girl to the right of her and raised it up. "Every other girl raise their hand, please." She waited for them to follow instructions. "Good, if your hand is up, please turn to your right and take hands with your partner." After a minute of confusion about right and left, there were four pairs joined. "Excellent. Hands down. There is a word in there, ingredients. Take half a minute and talk with your partner about what this word means."

Lily scanned the circle watching. She took note of the ones who either weren't talking or were trying to distract their partner. There were two girls, Moira and Anna. They did not know what the word meant. Anna was Mary's partner.

"Anna, can you tell us what Mary said?" Anna stuttered a little and looked caught. "Mary, could you whisper your answer in Anna's ear."

The group waited and then Anna smiled with her whole face. "It means things you mix together to make bread."

"Perfect, Anna! And thank you Mary, for your help!" Both girls smiled and raised their chins a bit. "Let's keep going. You are all coming along so well as readers!"

By noon, she had read with the girls, worked on arithmetic and geography with the boys, and they had all done a group lesson to create and build an oven that could bake a biscuit without a fire. They had to measure the ingredients, mix them and bake the biscuit. One of the boys suggested a magnifying glass to heat a small metal pan through an opening in a box. The biscuit was still a bit sticky on top, but otherwise edible. They had elected a particularly well-fed boy as the taster. He declared it good enough to keep you from starving.

169

"You have all earned some well-deserved play time. Let's break for lunch and I'll give you five extra minutes to play before I call you back." The kids cheered and ran for their lunch pails before filing out the door in a rush.

The door slammed and Lily watched the dust particles caught up in the dervish of air swirling toward the ceiling. The wood desks, exactly like ones she had seen in museums, glowed from the oil of many small hands over walnut striations. The room was so different from her classroom in 2018 but the children were the same. Different faces, different lives, but the unmistakable joy of learning and feeling accomplished resonated around the room.

The door opened and knocked her out of her reverie. Bettie stepped inside. She smiled like a school girl when her eyes adjusted and fell on Lily. "Oh, Lily. I just had to come to tell you. William and I need to take a brief trip to Lexington for William's business. You need to come, too. We certainly must do a little shopping and get some items for your wardrobe. Since, well, you know, you won't be receiving any trunks from Frankfort any time soon," she winked, "and you really need a few things."

"Lexington? When are you going?"

"William wants to leave first thing in the morning. Can you cancel school?"

Lily almost laughed out loud but caught herself. In her previous life, the thought of school being canceled because you needed time off to go shopping was comical. Then she realized there really weren't any substitutes here. "Well, I suppose so. Not many other options, huh?"

Bettie looked around the room distracted by her own memories, "Nobody will care. The parents will be glad to have the help at home."

Lily stared at her with confusion. That certainly was never the reaction she would have had in her own time if school was randomly canceled with no real notice. There would be furious calls by parents having to miss work to stay home to watch their kids. Politicians would chime in about poorly run school districts. Some accountant would have a fit because no federal funding would be received for that day.

"Times sure have changed," Lily mumbled.

"What dear?" Bettie turned to her.

"Oh, nothing. Just thinking about rearranging my lesson plan," Lily lied.

"Oh, I'm sure it won't be a bother. And we will have such a delightful time! We will actually be staying in Versailles not far from Lexington. We can visit my dear friend Suzanne. I haven't seen her since I spent two years at Sayre Female Institute as a young lady. You will love her."

"Sayre, you say?" Lily said, wondering if it's the same school in Lexington in the current time.

"Oh, yes. Those were the days. Teas and dresses and giggles. The days of girlhood. So different from today. For me, at least. I'm sure it's all the same for Susanne. Marrying William changed my life a great deal, but I'd have it no other way."

***

The train pulled up slowly at the station. The deafening cha cha chushhh of the steam escaping the powerful engine made Lily's ears ring. She had been on historic train rides where refurbished engines pulled weathered train cars to give you a taste of the past. Those train rides didn't compare to the real thing. The bright blue velvet seats, the wood trim

171

gleaming from layers of polish, even the engine which seemed just a little more powerful as it ate up track like a lion bounding across a field, it all gave her goosebumps. She sat next to Bettie who worked on needlepoint all the way there. William sat across from them in the bench seat. They faced each other as a grouping. Lily watched out the window and marveled at the neatly painted homes that dotted the hillsides as they came into town. Finally, the train stopped with a jolt that sent them swaying in their seats.

The conductor hollered out, "Versailles station!" He quickly strode down the center aisle to make his way to the next car.

"That is us, my dear," said William as he rose and offered her his hand to help her up. Bettie stowed her needlework in a tapestry bag which she slung over her arm before taking his hand.

"Are you ready, dear Lily?" Bettie offered, looking over her shoulder as she turned away from the window. Lily followed them to disembark.

On the platform, William tipped the conductor for getting their bags out of the storage compartment and carried them to the ladies. Bettie scoured the crowd for a glimpse of Suzanne.

"Bettie! Bettie! Is that you?" They heard a holler near them. Turning, they saw a woman hurrying along the rail with a gentleman following behind her.

"Suzanne! Look at you! It's been so long. Has it been six years?" The ladies hugged and then held each other's arms as they looked at each other.

"Yes, I believe it has. It was just after little Carlton was born. Now he is a half-grown little man!"

"Oh, I'd love to see him. Come to the inn for some refreshment and you can rest."

"That sounds lovely. Oh, Suzanne, I would like for you to meet our," she hesitated, "our cousin. This is Lily Wallingsford. She is staying with us a while."

Susannah looked her up and down and smiled. "Well, aren't you a pretty thing." She turned to Bettie, "Your cousin, you say?"

"Yes, it's a bit complicated, but yes. She is now engaged to our Mr. McEwen back at the farm. Do you remember him from my letters?"

"Yes! How wonderful! I surely can't wait to hear all the details. Let's make our way to the inn."

The group of five made their way to the carriage waiting in front of the station. Suzanne's husband, Edward climbed into the driver's seat and gave the reins a snap. The carriage pulled away and the clopping sounds of the horse's hooves filled her ears.

Lily had been to Versailles many times. It was just a short drive from Frankfort. She always enjoyed the lush green rolling hills of horse farms along US 60 that connected Frankfort to Versailles. The town seemed like a movie set with characters roaming around a movie-perfect, fake landscape of shops and businesses. A law office, a dry goods store, a post office all had their place. Several nice homes lined the street. They turned off the main street and an inn came into view. It was two stories with a large porch that wrapped around to the side. The side porch was screened in.

She felt an energy here. A warm tickling of excitement washed over her arms and up her neck. It felt magical but she couldn't figure out why.

William helped them out of the carriage and they stepped up onto the porch.

"Welcome to the Versailles Inn, ladies. I hope your stay is good," said Edward. He ushered them into the front room.

"I will speak to the kitchen about some light refreshment, if you will make yourselves at home." He disappeared down a hallway behind a staircase in the foyer.

They all sat and gave a sigh of relief that the journey was done. Suzanne discreetly looked over Lily when Lily was looking the other way. Lily could feel her eyes taking inventory. She wondered if there was something wrong with her clothes or whether Suzanne was just snobby.

"Suzanne, Lily and I were hoping to do some shopping in Lexington while we are here. Lily's bags were lost in an accident when she arrived. I have helped her with her wardrobe but she really needs a few things. Perhaps you could go with us? It would be fun!"

"An accident? Dear child, were you hurt? Was it awful?" Suzanne directed her questions to Lily.

The hairs on Lily's neck pricked up and she quickly reached to massage the back of her neck. "No, thank goodness. My carriage got swept away in the river. I'm not sure how it happened," she paused to think about the accident again, "but Bettie's farm hand, Mr. McEwen, pulled me out."

"How terrifying!" Suzanne kept staring at her. "I'm sorry to stare. You just, well, for some reason you remind me of my dear friend Everleigh. Perhaps you'll meet her while you are here."

"Oh, do I look like her?"

"Sort of, yes, but, it's the way you talk, really. Your casual lilt in your speech. And I suppose how you carry yourself."

Bettie watched Suzanne with curiosity. "Interesting. Yes, she does have a slightly different accent. Where is your friend Everleigh from?

"Charleston, actually." She gave an amused laugh. "I suppose her accent is very different. It's more the words she says."

"Suzanne, tell me how is your life? What have you and Edward been doing these days?" said Bettie.

"We run the inn. It does well. There are always customers. I have been helping my friend Everleigh with her school. She has a school for lunatics and retarded souls."

Lily cringed when she said retarded.

Suzanne noticed the discreet facial change, "Why you are just like her. She does the same thing. -Says that we should not call them lunatics. I don't know what else to call them, but Everleigh says they are," she paused thinking, "challenged. That's it."

Lily froze. Only a person from the modern time would use that word. "Challenged, you say?"

"Yes. Odd, isn't it?" said Suzanne.

"Certainly. I'd like to meet your friend. Could we visit her? Maybe I could see her school."

Bettie added, "Suzanne, Lily is a school teacher," nodding.

"How wonderful is that?" Suzanne's eyes lit up.

"Yes! She has been taking over at our Stephensport school while she is visiting. We were in the lurch when our last teacher ran for the hills."

Lily chuckled to herself. There have been many times over the last few years she wanted to just 'run for the hills.'

"Well, I'm certain we will see her soon," said Suzanne.

"See who, Suzanne? Are my ears ringing?" A delicate blond woman stepped into the parlor. She had a broad smile and an easy demeanor. Lily noticed right away this woman did not carry herself like the women of this time. Suzanne

175

jumped up and reached for the woman's hands before pulling her in for a kiss on the cheek.

"Why, you, darlin'. You're always the talk of the town, aren't you?" Both woman laughed at that.

"Well, that's just great. What have I done now?"

Lily rose to her feet, transfixed by this woman. Suzanne introduced her, "Everleigh, please meet my dear friend Bettie and her cousin Lily. Lily is her guest for a while and seems to think you and she would have a great deal in common."

Everleigh turned to Lily now with interest. She looked into her eyes, "Do I know you?"

"I don't think so, but we may have been to the same place once." Lily was careful to tiptoe around the conversation until she was certain.

"And where is that?"

"Oh, it's hard to get there. Or rather, it's hard to get here when you've been there."

"Is that so? And," she paused, "how did you get here from there?"

"A car accident." Lily threw the word car in there hoping to get her point across. If Everleigh was not a time traveler, her next question would be to ask what a car was.

"A *car* accident?" She now stared into Lily's eyes. "Were you hurt?"

"No, ma'am, but my car, I mean carriage, was swept away into the river. It was very confusing. I must have blacked out. I never felt the impact."

"I see. Well, we must talk more. Perhaps after tea we can take a walk in the garden. I would love to get to know you better."

***

176

They didn't say a word as they walked along the garden path. Lily stole a glance back toward the inn and turned to Everleigh. Everleigh put a finger to her lips to silently prompt her to stay quiet. They reached a bench near a pond where sprouts of grass hugged the edge.

"Okay," said Everleigh, "I think we are alone now." She looked intently at Lily as though answers would show through her skin.

"I'm from 2018," Lily whispered.

Everleigh's eyes opened a bit wider. "I," she started but then broke off.

"Are you a time traveler, too?"

"Yes, but," she broke off again.

"So, can we get back? When are you from?" Lily scrunched her mouth at her mangled grammar. "I mean, from what year are you?"

"I came from 2016, but it's complicated. This is not my body."

"Not your body? So you, too?" Lily took a step back.

Everleigh looked at her stunned. "Yes. I was in my thirties. I had a career in business consulting. My mother gave me a gift, a bar of soap that has a spell on it. When I bathed with it, it transported me back and in this body." She gestured to herself with her hand.

"Hm. Well, I was a teacher in 2018, in my thirties. I have no idea what caused the time travel. I careened off a bridge in my car and somewhere before hitting the water, I think the time and body change happened. My car sunk to the bottom of the Ohio River after I managed to get to the creek bank."

"Well, then. I guess there is more than one way to do it. I still have the bar of soap that has a spell on it. It caused me to travel back in time to this body. I always assumed I could use it again and go back, but I didn't want to. I love my life here."

"I see." Lily stopped breathing for a moment. "The only thing I can think of was that I had a sprig of a cedar branch tucked in my hair. I've mulled it around and I remember there was a legend about cedar trees being the tree of life and housing the spirits of ancestors. Maybe there is something to that. I really have no idea. So, are our bodies still back there? In the future?"

"I don't know. I guess since I don't need it anymore, I don't care. Maybe it died without my spirit. Maybe it's in a hospital somewhere being taken care of. I really don't know."

"Do you think it would work for me? The soap? I don't know how it all worked to get me here. One minute I was driving. I must have driven off the road. I hit a curb near the bridge. I remember the car careening through mid-air and then nothing. The car with me in it was sinking in the water. No boom. No splash. It's like that time in between was cut out or maybe I was in between."

"Fascinating. So, you want to go back? I mean, there is nothing here that holds your heart?"

Lily mulled her words in her mind. Her parents were back in 2018. How could she leave them, she wondered? She would never see them again. But, if she left this time period, how could she live without Evan? Their images blurred together making her head hurt.

"My parents," she paused, "they are the only family I have. But," she continued, "there's someone here that I've met. I love him."

A tear swelled and spilled. She couldn't choose. What kind of unfair God would make her choose this? Perhaps it was all beyond her control anyway and she was stuck here.

"Oh, sweetie, don't cry. We will figure this out. For now just enjoy your time here. That can't hurt anything, right?"

Lily nodded. "I'm so glad to have met you. I don't feel as alone."

"That's right. You're not alone. One thing I do know is that you aren't here by accident." Everleigh gave her a quick hug. "You and your friends must come to dinner at my house. We can visit more then. I'd love for you to meet my mom and dad. Dad is a whole other story that I will tell you about later."

"Your mom and dad? They time traveled, too?"

"Like I said, that's a whole other story."

"Well, that sounds great, Everleigh. Thanks so much. Meeting you has made me feel so much better."

Chapter 8 - Turn of the Century Church

William spent several days on his business and Lily and Bettie rarely saw him. They enjoyed shopping in Versailles and spending time at Suzanne's Inn.

William and Bettie were having coffee on the porch. The golden morning light poked through the white trellis, highlighting indigo blue morning glories.

"A letter came this morning that was penned by the elder of the church in Stephensport, Mr. Ames. Do you know of him?" said William.

"Yes. His wife is a dreadful woman. I know her from the quilting bee."

"Apparently, he is becoming ever more vociferous about Lily teaching the girls to read. He would like a full review of her curriculum as soon as we return."

"I'm not surprised. His own wife can't sneeze without getting prior permission. What's worse is she seems to think herself fortunate to the point of being holier than anyone else because she is married to the domineering deacon." Bettie pushed out her lips into a pucker and rolled her eyes.

"Whatever Mrs. Ames thinks, it matters not. Mr. Ames could make it very difficult for Lily. He has a great deal of authority over the town. Many feel that if the lower class women learn to read, our whole way of life will be jeopardized. They fear that women won't be satisfied to raise a family and keep a home."

Lily had stepped onto the veranda just in time to hear his comment.

She interjected, "And is it better for a woman to never realize her full potential? What if all men were saddled like oxen to pull a plow all their life. Would not the men who are good at law or preaching miss their calling? Lumping a whole group of people into one pot is not utilizing their God-given abilities."

"Oh, Lily!" He stood out of respect as she approached the table. "Please join us." He stepped around the table to pull out her chair. I'll have another place setting brought out. Excuse me." He went inside the inn.

"So how did this conversation come up?" Lily asked.

"Well, the town council is getting their dander up because you are teaching the girls to read. Apparently you are going to have all those girls running off and taking men's jobs next." Bettie smiled at her.

"I see. If they are more qualified then maybe the men should move over."

"You and I know that, but you may be messing with very old ways of thinking." Bettie winked at her.

They both sat in silence a minute before Bettie continued, "It's not that you aren't doing the right thing. It's all about how you can present it so that the men think it was their idea."

"That's a tall order, Bettie."

"It is, but it's not impossible."

"I'm curious as to how much of this is coming from Brian Everbright, as well."

William returned with a server in tow. The server placed a coffee cup on a saucer and poured her fresh coffee.

Bettie turned to William, "What do you think Lily should do?"

"I'm not sure. There was a time when I had no issue with the way our school taught all the children. As I have been around Lily more, I'm not sure I'm comfortable anymore. Perhaps we are doing a disservice to the young ladies of Stephensport."

"William! It pleases me greatly to hear you say that. I was worried about what you would say about my plans for today, but now I am more certain than ever. I would like to take Lily shopping in Lexington and to visit some of my old friends from Sayre. I've heard that some are making groundbreaking headway at settlement schools in the mountains."

William's forehead creased. "Be careful, darling. While I agree with the direction Lily is going, I also know that change doesn't come easy." He looked at Lily with a clenched jaw. "There will be resistance."

"Now, William, we are just going visiting. We won't stir up too much trouble."

"Visiting is fine. I just know what the ramification of the visits can be."

Bettie smiled at him innocently and batted her eyelashes. "I'm sure I have no idea what you mean."

He pulled her hand closer so that he could kiss her cheek. "Still darling, use caution."

***

After breakfast, Bettie and Lily boarded a carriage that took them to Lexington.

"Lily, we have been invited to tea at my friend Eileen's home. I haven't seen her in years since we were in school together at Sayre. I really think you'll adore her. She's smart as a whip. She's friends with Mary Desha and, my word, that woman can get a bee in her bonnet! Apparently she is in a tizzy about how the government is letting people live in Alaska with little to nothing. She's been teaching there for about a year."

"She ran a school didn't she?" Lily remembered from a DAR meeting presentation.

"Yes. You've heard of her, then. She and her mother had a fine school. Then she worked for the schools in Lexington. She was supposed to be back from Alaska soon, but I don't know if she is yet."

The carriage ride was long and by the time they got to the edge of Lexington, Lily's stomach was growling. Her back ached from the hard wooden seat and all the bouncing as the wheels hit ruts. She glanced at Bettie and saw she was lost in thought.

"I'm pretty well tired of this carriage ride," she offered up.

Bettie focused back on reality, "Oh sure. It's a long ride. You must be getting tired. Eileen will put out a nice spread for us, I'm sure."

That sounded nice. Lily thought about how that would play out. She thought about the times her friends had come over and they would just go to the Mexican restaurant. *"No one put out any spread,"* she chuckled to herself.

The carriage pulled up a narrow street lined with Victorian homes. Every house had freshly painted trim accenting perfect stone masonry with sparkling windows. It was the most perfectly kept historic street she had ever seen, except it wasn't historic yet.

The carriage slowed and they pulled to the curb in front of a two-story home. Black doors flanked with topiary trees rose above the front stairs. Lily saw a face dart from the window just before the doors swung open. A tiny woman glided down the steps followed by a tall man in a black suit trying to keep up. Lily assumed he must be a butler the way the woman nearly ran over him to get out the door.

The carriage rocked as the driver disembarked. Lily reached for a handle to steady herself. She was more convinced than ever that shock absorbers were invented as a necessity after life in this bumpy world. The carriage door swung open with a squeak of the hinge and a man's hand presented itself.

"You go ahead, Bettie. I don't know her." Lily said softly.

"Oh, honey, she will love you. Don't you worry." Bettie sprang up and took the man's hand. Then all at once, she slowed down and lightly stepped from the carriage.

Lily took her lead and did the same after taking the butler's hand. Eileen was tiny. Lily couldn't get over how small everyone was in this time.

The two ladies hugged and laughed at the delight of seeing each other again. "Oh, my word, Bettie, how long has it been?" Eileen said.

"Too long! Would you look at how you haven't aged a day?" said Bettie.

"Now, Bettie, four babies have had their way with my figure since I saw you last. So you keep your indulging words to yourself!"

The two of them held both hands and looked at each other. "Eileen, it's wonderful to see you again!" Bettie beamed with delight.

Turning to Lily, "Introduce me to your friend? I can't wait to meet her!" said Eileen.

Bettie reached for Lily to bring her in close, "This is my sweet cousin Lily from Frankfort. She has been staying with us a while. She's been teaching at the school. And," she stretched out the word, "she is engaged to my vigorous farm hand, Evan McEwen." Bettie winked at Lily and then made a duck lips expression at Eileen.

Both of them smiled with wide eyes and took Lily by the hand. They acted like giddy school girls laughing and hugging.

Eileen became the voice of reason, "Well, you both must be famished and worn out. I have a nice buffet set out for you to refresh yourself and then we will have a good visit. Let's go inside." She motioned for them to make their way inside.

The buffet was grander than any dinner buffet Lily had ever been to. Besides the dizzying array of food, the china and silverware were like something you would only see in a museum. Each piece of silverware looked like it was hand crafted into a unique shape with scrolled leaves and beaded designs. The china plates looked hand-painted with scenes of 18th century lovers walking in gardens and meadows. The closest thing she could associate it to was the elaborate DAR teas back when she was a junior member. Even so, they were a pale comparison to this.

The footman stood before Bettie with a plate and then waited. Lily watched to know what to do. Bettie would point at what she wanted and the footman would spoon some onto her plate. The footman took her plate to the table and then helped her to be seated. The footman did the same for Lily. Lastly, Eileen sat with them at the table with her plate. Lily hoped her modern good manners were good enough. She followed Bettie's lead hoping she wouldn't make a ghastly social faux pas.

They ate with light conversation until they were all satisfied and then retired to the sun room. The bright light from the windows and yellow striped fabric on the chairs gave the room a cheerful feeling.

When they all settled into their chairs, Eileen started the conversation, "So tell me about high society in Stephensport. What's new there?"

Bettie paused and Lily understood now how much Bettie's life had changed. Bettie had very little social life, certainly not anything as nice as even this visit, so far. "Well, darlin'," Bettie started. "You know, I'm so busy with Carlton and the house, I hardly have time for socials."

Eileen gave Bettie a heavy look of pity.

"Don't you start with that sympathy look. You know that I chose my life. I chose William despite all convention. And we are fine. It's just a different life than how it was. I love my William with all my heart and wouldn't trade one minute of my life for something else. As far as I'm concerned, I am the most fortunate woman alive."

"I'm sorry, Bettie. I just wish you could have William *and* the life to which you were accustomed."

"I understand that. I really do. But don't waste a tear on that. I am the happiest I have ever been." She smiled with her whole face and Lily knew she was telling the truth.

"All right then, so now tell me, Lily, how is it going at your school?"

Bettie interjected, "Now don't sugar-coat it, darlin'. Eileen is well aware of the struggles in education.

Lily wished she could hear about Eileen's struggles before she got into the frustrations of Stephensport. "Where to start? My biggest hurdle right now is getting the parents to believe that girls need to learn to read and write as much as the boys do."

Apparently, that was all Eileen needed to commiserate. Her eyes rolled back in her head and she rested her wrist on her forehead. "Don't I know it? If I had a penny for every time I have said that, I could open a free boarding school for every girl in this state!"

"So even here, in the city, you have the same issues?" Lily shook her head.

"Oh, most certainly. The wealthy girls get a fine education at private schools. The less fortunate girls are lucky to get past primary before they are pulled out. These families don't realize there's so much more these girls could be doing besides laundry or cooking."

"Right!"

"Of course even if they did get through a complete education, it's an uphill battle to get any man to realize they really can handle the work, though."

"It's hard to believe how far we've come," Lily mumbled to herself thinking of the twenty-first century.

"How far we've come? I don't think we have gotten anywhere. What do you mean?" Eileen asked.

"Oh! Right! I was being sarcastic."

Eileen lowered her lids and looked down her nose at Lily skeptically. "You're an odd girl, Lily."

"I suppose I am. Sorry."

Bettie interjected, "Now Eileen, she's just tired. It's been difficult in Stephensport. She has tried very hard to teach the girls to read and write and, even though the girls are all up for it, the parents and the town council is pitching a fit. William got a letter today from the council that said if she didn't return to the previous curriculum, she was going to be asked to resign."

"What are they so afraid of? Do they think the girls will take over the town?" said Lily.

"That's exactly what they think. Women will be taking men's jobs to start with and before you know it, women won't even want to get married," said Bettie.

"They don't give themselves much credit, do they? I mean, are they that afraid of relying on a girl falling in love with them instead of just needing their money?" said Eileen.

The door opened quickly, banging into the chair railing molding on the wall with a crack. All three women jumped in their seats. Eileen sprang from her chair to see what happened.

A well-dressed man strode around the corner giving them all a cursory glance before spouting, "Eileen dear, I can't be disturbed just now. You and your little friends will have to visit another time. I need quiet." He pressed his lips together in annoyance.

"Of course dear," Eileen curtseyed with a bob before turning back to Lily and Bettie, "Perhaps, you wouldn't mind if I took them over to the Deshas' for a while. I promise to be home before supper."

It was a combination of asking him and her guests at the same time. Her husband didn't bother to look at her while she spoke.

"You can do as you please as long as I am not disturbed," he said as he headed toward the study.

Lily felt bad for her. He treated her like the hired help.

"Thank you, ladies. Bernard has a demanding job. He isn't always like that."

"No problem, Eileen. I would love to meet Mary Desha if she is home. What a treat!"

Eileen smiled gratefully. "Then let's be on our way!"

***

188

Before long they were ushered into Miss Desha's drawing room. They sat on the delicately curved chairs with blue velvet cushions welted into the dark wood.

"I had no idea she was back before the other day," whispered Eileen. "She wasn't there as long as she planned apparently. I've been meaning to pay her a visit to see what happened."

A flurry of light footsteps was heard coming down the hall and the door opened wide. Lily tried to size up where the energy came from. The small woman stood before them with a warm smile as though she were delighted her best friends had come over. From what Eileen said about not knowing if Mary was in town, she knew Eileen could not have been a close friend. And yet, Mary appeared genuinely pleased to see them.

"Ladies! Welcome! I am so glad you are here. Your timing couldn't be more perfect. I was just about to have tea and I really could use your input on something I am mulling over."

"Oh, Mary! You are such a dear. I'd like to introduce my good friend Sarah Elizabeth Black. She's called Bettie. She and I attended Transylvania Female Institute together, now Sayre, of course. And this is her cousin Lily Wallingsford. Lily is Bettie's cousin from Frankfort and a school teacher."

Mary didn't miss a beat and smiled broadly at them both. "Well, am I just the luckiest lady ever to have you visit me? Please make yourselves at home. I can't wait to hear all about your adventures."

Lily immediately felt at ease. Mary Desha made her feel like they were long lost friends who'd been apart far too long. She marveled at the difference between hearing a lecture about a notable person in history or even watching an actor recreate a person versus being here in front of the real celebrity in the living and breathing flesh.

The four of them settled around a round table near the window overlooking a small garden with brick walls. Sparrows flitted around a bird bath outside under the long delicate dark arms of a Redbud tree with pink lavender blooms sprouting along every limb.

"My dear, Lily, how does your classroom in Stephensport fair?" Mary searched her eyes as though this was crucial information.

Lily swallowed hard, "The children are wonderful, eager to learn."

Mary looked at her with a steadfastness that unsettled Lily. She clasped her hands in her lap to keep from fidgeting.

"That's the first hurdle and it seems you have crossed it well. What is the real issue?"

"It's the town. They think I am taking the girls away from their chores if I keep them at school too long. Or worse, if I teach them to read and do arithmetic, that the girls will be unmarriageable."

"I see. Yes. Marriage isn't the end all. I have managed myself quite well and plan to continue in this fashion without a husband. I do wish girls were not compelled to saddle themselves into a marriage at the first opportunity. That's just my opinion. To each, her own."

Bettie shot a glance at Eileen.

Mary continued, "However, you must persist in training the girls to think and read and do arithmetic. I can only venture to guess that a women who can think must be far more appealing than one who requires constant instruction for the simplest endeavor. Perhaps if you were to show how an educated female would be an asset to a man? Meet them at their level of thinking. If the townspeople can only find good in marrying off their daughters, then sell them on how an educated mind is a better investment for a man."

"That's a direction I have not tried. It would be a compromise."

"And if that won't work, we can just start our own school for girls and hide them away."

Lily, Bettie and Eileen's eyes got as big as saucers.

"I'm not serious, ladies! A little humor, that's all. Of course it might move things along faster but I suppose we should refrain from kidnapping." She laughed at her own joke.

"So, Mary," said Eileen, "what are your plans now? Will you be going back to Alaska?"

She sighed, "I think not. Talk about some difficult people. Now, don't misunderstand, there are lovely people in Sitka. The governor and his wife were a delight. However, the parents at the school didn't share my opinion of how to handle mischievous little boys." She shook her head. "No, it was a grand experience for which I am grateful, however, I will pursue other endeavors. I have a friend in Washington, D.C. that may be able to find me a post. She has connections in the Pension Office. I expect to get word any day now. I really feel like great things are coming for women in this country and it will start there in the heart of democracy."

Lily smiled. "I'm sure you're right, Mary. Its women like you that will lay the foundation of equality for all women."

Mary looked at Lily as though lost in thought, finally answering, "It is only with great determination and zeal that we will ever make progress. We need a compass which will keep us from wavering on the journey. I'm still searching for it, and I believe it will come soon. Then we will hold it steadfastly and move forward."

Lily smiled. The future of the Daughters of the American Revolution was sitting in front of her, still in Mary Desha's mind. The other three founders were out there somewhere and within a year, they would come together and it would be born from their passion for this country and the desire to make a difference as women. History was happening right in front of her eyes.

"Mary, if I could teach the girls in my school one thing, what would you say is the most important?" said Lily.

"Oh now, let me think." She drummed her fingers while she thought. "Yes, I have it! You must teach them to keep within them the spirit of freedom upon which this country was founded, and to forever continue learning so that they will have an enlightened opinion to secure the blessings of liberty for themselves and their children. Yes, that is what's most important."

What a charge! Thought Lily. She thought Mary might say teach them literacy or teach them logic. This was a much greater mission than she had endeavored to fulfill before. She had tried to help them fully self-actualize through opportunity that education could bring. This was more of a mission that would set in motion a revolution of its own. *It's so much more than helping them become a doctor or a business owner.*

Armed with this directive, Lily knew what she had to do. She couldn't back down. She already knew where the country was going to be going. It wasn't like she would be alone in her thinking. Even though the town might not be ready for progressive education, the country was.

She turned to see Bettie eyeing her, "Looks like you got your marching orders, Lily," said Bettie.

Lily nodded.

"Then we will strap on our helmets and get going."

When they left that afternoon, Lily watched Mary Desha wave them off from her front porch. It was so hard to believe she had spent the afternoon with her, in her home, sipping tea and discussing patriotism and the cost of liberty.

It seemed so simple to Mary. The "self" movement of the twentieth century seemed so petty from this side. Not that there wasn't good reason to follow one's dreams like Evan had coming to America, but to make everyone's dream come true, she realized people must never cease to strive for intelligent citizenship in order to keep this democracy going.

They went by Eileen's and gave her a tearful goodbye. Then the carriage turned toward Versailles and began the long trip to the Versailles Inn. As they left the edge of the city of Lexington, Lily's thoughts turned to Evan. She missed him. She wondered what he would think of her ideas for teaching the girls in Stephensport. Her thoughts muddled together as images of him beside her on the blanket under the tree crept into her mind. She could feel the heat of his touch in her mind as she remembered. She closed her eyes and lost herself in the day dream.

"You getting tired, darlin'?" Bettie's voice crept into Lily's daydream.

"What?" Lily's eye's batted open. "Oh, I suppose so." She lied.

Bettie smiled. "You don't have to fool me, honey. It hasn't been that long since I was a smitten young girl." She paused a minute. "Oh wait. I still am!" she laughed at herself.

***

193

At the Versailles Inn, Everleigh and Malcolm joined them for dinner. Malcolm and Everleigh hung on each other's words. They couldn't keep their hands off each other.

"You all still act like newlyweds!" Lily laughed.

Everleigh smiled and said, "I feel like we are. The feeling never fades." She turned and looked at Malcolm who had the same dewy look on his face.

"I hate to tear you both apart, but I wanted to speak to Everleigh privately if that's okay," Lily said.

"Oh, sure! Come on. Let's sit on the porch." Everleigh kissed Malcolm and then she and Lily filed out of the dining room.

They settled into a wicker love seat before Everleigh asked, "So what's up?"

"I just wanted to get your opinion."

"Sure thing!"

"I am going to change up the way girls are being taught at the public school in Stephensport. I really feel like it would make a difference. The town council and the families are against it. I just don't think they see the value of the girls being able to read and write."

"Well, that's it, then. You need to show them it makes a difference."

"But how?" Lily asked.

"I got a lot of flack when I started the school for the disabled kids. The whole town and even some politicians wanted me to quit. They wanted to hide those kids away. I started by teaching them to do simple jobs that help others. I talked to some of the business owners and got them to sponsor a student to work at their business a few hours a day. As people saw the students doing good work and being productive, they eventually got used to them. There are still some who will never come around to progressive thinking, but many people aren't afraid of the students anymore. They are even friendly to them. And the students are so much happier than languishing in an asylum."

"Hm. I never thought of it on those terms."

"It really comes down to fear. The people who make the rules are afraid. Help them see how teaching the girls will help them and it will work out."

Part III

Chapter 9 – The Way Things Seem

Evan met them in the wagon at the train station in Stephensport. Lily saw him immediately when the train approached the curve into town. She couldn't miss him. His broad shoulders and wavy hair lifting with the breeze made him look like an angel that could protect her from anything. She wondered what he was thinking as he sat there. Two vertical creases between his eyebrows gave him a troubled look.

The wheels of the train squealed with the brakes. Lily gripped the cushion to keep from sliding off her seat. A final lurch forward of her body punctuated the end of the train ride as they came to a complete stop.

"Home again!" Bettie whispered to Lily.

By the time they made it to the platform, Evan had their cases in the wagon. He stepped forward to greet them and gave Lily a hopeful smile of welcome. Kissing her hand, he didn't say anything. Lily got the distinct feeling he was holding back.

He turned to William, "Do you mind if Lily and I walk? We will be home shortly."

She looked at him with a furloughed brow. The wagon pulled away and left them alone. The street was quiet in the mid-morning hour. Evan held out his arm for her and she looped her hand behind and through.

"It's good to see you. I missed you." She attempted to bridge the gap she felt from him.

"Yes. Certainly. Good to see you. Was it a good trip?"

"Very much. Has anything happened here? William spoke of a letter from the elders."

"Ah. Yes. I have heard rumblings in town."

"Are you worried?"

"About the rumblings, not really. People grumble. That's nothing unusual."

She turned to face him, stopping him from moving forward. "What is it then? What's the matter?"

"That's why I needed to talk to you. Brian has been busy. He hired a man to go to Frankfort. He has proof there is no Mr. and Mrs. Wallingsford at the address you gave. In fact there is no house there. It's a vegetable garden."

"How do you know he did this?"

"He confronted me."

"What?"

"He is very pleased with himself. He gave me the opportunity to get out of his way. He felt quite magnanimous about it. He threatened to sue William for everything he has as well as publicly humiliate all of us. Oh, and he reminded me that his influence is quite strong with the judge at the county seat in Hardinsburg."

"Oh, dear Lord. William will be devastated. What did you say?"

"I told him I didn't care what information he had. He could not hold us hostage and tear us apart."

"Okay. What did he say about that?"

"He laughed in my face and walked away. That's not all, though. I have an itchy feeling that the attack on the riverboat may have something to do with him. I keep going over it in my head. Then I saw in the Courier Journal that the men that were captured have made a plea deal. Apparently overtaking the boat and causing its demise was not their intention. They are singing like a bird."

"Evan! That's a big accusation. Have they specifically mentioned Brian being involved?"

"His name hasn't been mentioned in the paper but I'm wondering if this is how he knows I was not in Frankfort."

"So he is using his authority in town to get his way and hoping this story doesn't get out." Lily thought.

He continued, "The day after he tried to intimidate me, I heard the elders had met and they were starting a witch hunt for you."

"So, it was him!"

"Lily, he will tear William and Bettie to pieces and disgrace you until your only option is to acquiesce to his demands. Then he will have you under his thumb."

She thought about his words without any expression until, at last, she straightened. "I think not. I'm not accustomed to being under anyone's thumb. I need to think about how to deal with this, but I know one thing for certain. I didn't get this far in life by laying down and letting people walk on me. Besides, if he is that dirty, the truth will come out."

He searched her eyes, taking in the soft skin of her cheeks and delicate lips. "Lily, how old are you?"

His question caught her off guard and she laughed. "Oh, sweetheart, I suppose you think I'm about twenty. I can't lie. I'm a bit older than that.

"I guess looking young runs in your family."

"No. That's not what I'm talking about. I haven't said anything because it was just too weird."

He looked at her with a scrunched brow.

"The time travel wasn't the only supernatural event. I don't understand it, but somehow, my body didn't travel with me."

His mouth parted slightly like he was looking for the words to say. "But, you have a body." He reached out and took her hand.

She squeezed his hand back but pulled it away. Her breath quickened as her nerves made a heavy feeling in her chest. "Somehow in my mysterious journey here, I landed in a different body. My soul is thirty-two."

He stood there with wide eyes.

"I know. It's crazy. I'm sorry if you feel deceived."

"Thirty-two! Were you--. Ah," he stammered. "Were you married?"

"Oh! No. I never married. Not that I didn't want to. It just didn't work out."

"I see. That's a relief. You're *much* older than me. I'm just twenty-six."

"That's not much of a difference, right? And," she held her arm out gracefully to look at it. "I'm much better looking." She realized what that sounded like and clarified, "Not better looking than you. Better looking than my old body."

He turned his back to her and put his hands on his hips.

"What is it? Are you mad at me?" She darted around him to face him.

He looked away. "I need some time. This is too much to take in. I, I need to think. Let's just get you home."

He gripped her elbow firmly but gently and led her down the sidewalk.

Annoyed with his prodding, she shook herself free and crossed her arms, walking next to him silently. Perhaps she had been too glib about this little fact that she hadn't told anyone. She could understand how he might feel betrayed. Believing her story about being from another time was hard enough for anyone. Add to that the fact that she was actually someone else than meets the eye and you had a hard pill to swallow. She relaxed a bit and let her arms fall naturally to her sides as she walked.

She stole a glance at him from the corner of her eye. He was staring dead ahead expressionless. "Evan."

He didn't respond and kept walking.

"Evan!" She reached for his hand.

"Don't touch me. I don't know who you are."

"Evan! I'm me. Did you fall in love with me or my face?"

He stopped and stared at her before speaking. "Generally, one doesn't have make a difference. The face and the person are one and the same."

"Okay. I'll give you that. But I'm still the same person in here." She pointed to her heart.

He sighed and looked down. "Look. I just need some time."

"What does that mean? Do you still want to marry me?" A tear rolled off her cheek as she said the words.

"Lily, or whatever your name is, I don't know. There is the house." He nodded in that direction. They stood near the drive to Black's Farm. "Let me be for a time."

"Lily. My name is Lily. Evan! I love you." She tried to reach for him again, but he brushed her off and stepped away.

With a grimace, he turned and dashed away before she could say anything else. She was standing there alone, arms folded against her chest, crying. Alone again, just like with Andrew. Her heart twisted inside.

"My dearest Lily. Whatever could be the matter? I saw the dashing hillbilly run away. Too much pressure?" Brian stood about ten feet away with a smirk.

She wiped away her tears with the palm of her hand. "No! It's really none of your business."

He stepped closer and gave her a charitable smile. "It's quite all right. You have no need to fear. I can make it all fine. Do you really want a husband that runs off when the going gets tough?"

"You have no idea. If I told you the truth, you couldn't handle it."

"The truth? Fascinating. You are so intriguing. Come now, Lily." He caressed her cheek with the back of his hand. "I have the means to fulfill your every dream. Why do you fight it?" He dropped his hands and relaxed his shoulders. "Honestly, Lily. Why can't you see that I only want to love you."

She relaxed her arms, too. "Brian, I'm sure you're sincere, in your own twisted way. It's just that I'm not sure your kind of love is good for me."

He looked around and she realized she was out of view of the house. No one could see them. His arm shot around her waist and his mouth was on her ear before she could try to get free.

"That's the thing about women, they never know what's good for them." He kissed her neck, alternating small bites and kisses down to her shoulder.

Yet, again, her body betrayed her and her knees started to buckle. A part of her heart wanted him. She felt like she could let go and let him take over and it would all be alright. He seemed so capable.

While he gripped her waist with one arm, his other hand locked around her wrists so that she couldn't move. She lost

202

her balance and lost her footing in the damp leaves underfoot. The shift in weight pulled him forward and they fell to the ground. Trying to catch himself so he didn't fall on top of her, he let go of her hands and reached for the ground. She tried to grab at the tree branches of the cedar tree beside them and only managed to break off a stem.

For a brief moment, they were suspended in the air and all sound stopped. No birds chirping. No wind in the trees. The next minute she was on the ground with a teenage boy on top of her. There was no thud of hitting the cold dirt.

"What are you two doing there? Get a room! Good grief!" An older man in jeans and a tee shirt stood a few feet away with a broom.

Brian rolled off her and stood up in one motion. He offered his hand. "Lily, please forgive—," He broke off when he looked at her. "Who are you?"

She looked down at her clothes. She was wearing jeans and a pair of Converse sneakers. She reached up and felt short crunchy spiky hair.

"Who are you?" She stood up and looked in his eyes. "What—"

"This is most irregular. I will not suffer such humiliation," the boy said as he straightened and place his fists on his hips.

She knew that posture. It was Brian. She looked past the man and saw down the street. There were no stores, banks, or an inn. Cars were parked in driveways. The road was paved with faded black asphalt.

"Oh no. No. This can't happen. Not now." She looked at Brian who was alternately staring at her and an old man walking toward them. He hadn't realized he had changed yet.

"You kids need to get on outta here, ya' hear?" The man must have felt like his point was made because he turned and walked away muttering to himself.

Lily stood up. "Brian, look at me. Don't look at anything but me."

"What? I'm not accustomed to taking orders from a--, Are you a girl?" His eyes landed on her breasts. "Is your hair… purple?"

"A girl. I understand your confusion, but I need to tell you something. We--, we--." She couldn't get it out. How could he understand?

"What are you trying to say?" At that moment a red diesel Dodge truck crossed the bridge over Sinking Creek and sped past them at twenty-five miles an hour. Brian turned and watched it travel down Main Street.

"What in the world?" He left her now and walked to the edge of the road. He stopped there and toed the black pavement with his shoe. He put his fists on his hips and looked down the length of Main Street, squinting his eyes. He turned and looked back at the metal bridge with diagonal and arching blue-gray supports with bolts and nuts. Utterly confused, he looked back at her.

"What in the world?" said Brian.

"Welcome to 2018. Stephensport, one hundred and twenty-eight years in the future. This is why you couldn't find my parents in Frankfort. They, nor me, had not been born yet."

"Your parents? I don't even know you. I don't believe any of this. Where is Lily?" He brushed her off with a wave of his hand.

"Oh, it's true alright. I'm Lily. Have you looked at yourself?"

He looked down at his clothes, a black tee shirt with three parallel rips across the chest meant to look like a monster had attacked him, dark blue skinny jeans, and a pair of black Converse sneakers.

"Oh! Oh my word." His eyebrows were arched high. He went pale and she wondered if he would actually faint. "But-. How?"

She looked down trying to think of how to explain something that she couldn't figure out either. The broken cedar twig lay in the dirt. The sound came to her ears suddenly as though it was affirming what she couldn't imagine was true. The same sound she had heard from the window in her room in 1889, the low clear one like a wet finger around the edge of a wine glass.

She knelt down on her knee and picked up the flat green bit of cedar. Raising it to her nose, she breathed in the clear woodsy scent. It brought back the memory of cedar blocks in her chest of drawers back in Frankfort.

"This." She said twirling the spring between her fingers. A light breeze wafted through her spikey hair giving her chills. She shivered rubbing her arms.

"What? What do you mean this? A piece of a tree? What is that supposed to mean?"

"I suspected it, but wasn't convinced until now. There is a legend that the cedar tree holds the souls of our ancestors. It's the tree of life. When I crossed over to 1889, I had been to the cemetery to talk to my grandmother's spirit. I found a sprig of this in the dirt and tucked it into my hair because it smelled nice. Reminded me of the past. Now here it is again. I was trying to break my fall and grabbed at a tree and ripped it out. It must be what carried us through time."

He stared at her with his mouth open. "Are you daft? Are you saying a tree branch took us to the future?"

If they were in the future, she knew she had to get back to her apartment. She looked toward the bridge to see if she saw her car. Maybe it was still there.

"Hold on," she told him.

"Hold on to what? And I am to assume that you are actually Lily?" He followed her as she walked toward the bridge.

"Yes. I'm Lily. Same old me. Just different body. Apparently bodies don't time travel well." She stepped onto the concrete bridge and walked along the side holding the top metal railing. Shadows of cross beams flitted over her face. She stepped up onto the narrow curbing, not quite wide enough to use as a sidewalk, but big enough to stand on and look over the side. The muddy creek water swirled past underneath. No car could be seen in the mud.

"I say, this is a rather sturdy construction, isn't it?"

"Well, the state does its best to make good bridges these days. No more wooden bridges." She sighed with resolution. "We need some money. Apparently my car washed away or something. I don't know. But we need to get to my apartment. In Frankfort."

"Whatever for?"

"Well, Mr. Everbright, we can't just sleep here on the side of the road, can we? And I need to figure out how to get us back to 1889. But before we go, I need to do something. If I'm never going to see my parents again, I at least want to say goodbye."

"Don't be ridiculous. I have plenty of money. Let's just go to the bank." He looked down the road and wrinkled up his brow.

"So you are starting to see the problem?"

"Where is the mercantile? Where is the bank and the inn? Where is my house, for heaven's sake?"

"It's all gone. Business here dried up long before I was even born. Nearly a hundred years ago. Your house, if it's still standing, likely has new owners. I would guess your family moved away when the railroad moved much of its work to Hardinsburg."

"Then what about my money?"

"I think it's safe to say, for the time being anyway, you don't really have any money. I suppose we could try to find your descendants but they will think you're a crackpot looking to make a buck off them."

If anybody could look so instantly dejected, she hadn't seen it. It was a hard fall to bear. She actually felt pity for him, especially since he looked like such a delinquent.

"Come on, look through your pockets. Maybe these two twits we fell into had some cash on them."

He reluctantly pulled his pockets inside out. He had a joint, some pills, a wrapped condom, and a $50 bill. "What's this? He held his hand up with the pocket contents.

"That would be illegal drugs, birth control, and cash. We will toss the drugs and keep the cash. You can put the condom back in your pocket. Good job!" She tossed the joint and the pills over the side of the bridge.

He turned pale again. "Birth control? What in the world do you do--" he broke off embarrassed. "I don't think I care for the future much."

"You'll be fine." She was glad he was stunned into a cooperating attitude, but she wondered how long it would be until the real Brain came out.

"And I must say, darling, you look ghastly."

"And there he is," she thought. She turned her thoughts to how she would get home. No public transportation came through here anymore. It was a good three hour's drive to

Frankfort. They couldn't walk it. She had no phone. All there was in town was a post office.

"Who is there?" He looked around.

She ignored him. "A post office. I guess that will have to do. It's better than mailing a letter from 1889."

"What? You want to send a letter?" He asked.

"Yeah, I think so. Come with me." She turned and headed toward the other end of Main Street. They reached the metal building that served as a post office. "I guess I can't leave you here on the street."

He puffed up at her words.

"Give me the fifty dollars," she asked.

"Excuse me?" he asked with wide eyes.

"I need to buy some stationary and a stamp, for heaven's sake! Do you think it's rightfully yours since it was in your ripped jeans?"

"Fifty dollars is a rather large sum of money for you to be handling." He fumbled in his pocket and pulled out the bill. She just glared at him.

"Thank you." She shoved it in her pocket and pushed the door open. The postal clerk sat behind the counter. It was not nearly as glorious as the post office in 1889 that had turned trim accents and polished wood counters. She decided that at some point in history we'd given up making public offices nice. Maybe it was too costly, but it's like we stopped respecting the public domain.

"Excuse me. I would like to buy a piece of paper and an envelope and a stamp." The clerk gave her a packaged set with an envelope that already had postage printed on it.

"That'll be $4.75, ma'am."

Brian gasped. "Good Lord! That's a week's salary for one of my clerks!"

"Shh!" Then she whispered to him, "Please don't say anything."

He looked at her mortified. Apparently, her 2018 modern woman self was more than he could handle.

She thanked the clerk and put the change in her pocket. She walked over to a side counter and picked up a pen. She noticed her fingernails were bitten down to the quick. She wrote out a quick letter, dashing a tear that was close to falling from her cheek. She folded the paper, inserted it and licked the envelope. She wrote out the address on the front. Brian read the address over her shoulder.

"There really is a Mr. and Mrs. Wallingsford in Frankfort, then." He asked.

"Yes. Now there is, anyway."

"I had somehow concluded in my mind that you were a tramp looking to find a golden goose."

She snorted, "Well, I guess I'm glad you have come to the conclusion I'm not that!"

His eyes narrowed, "Makes no difference, really, except that I'm glad to know that when I have you, you will be better than a dressed up tramp."

She coughed trying to catch her breath. He still thought a lot of himself, she thought to herself. She handed the sealed envelope to the clerk and they stepped back outside.

"Okay, then. How do we get back?" she wondered out loud.

"Get back? You mean to our time?"

"Yes. I know the sprig of greenery is needed but apparently holding it isn't enough or I would have disappeared when I picked it up off the ground." She fished the sprig from her back pocket."

"Give me that." He swiped it from her hand. "You're not going anywhere."

He proceeded to wave it around in the air in front of him. He gave a frustrated sigh and waved it over his head. Giving up, he said, "This is pointless. I am really beginning to believe you're batty."

"How else would you explain it, Einstein?" She crossed her arms and leaned back on her heels.

"Einstein? Why did you call me that? Who is Einstein?"

"While you play with that sprig, I'm going to think for a minute. She walked behind the post office to sit in the shade and look at the Ohio River going by. Brian followed her a few steps behind. She sat on a bench near a back door.

She had two instances to compare. The first time she had the sprig and crashed the car. She expected to felt an impact and there was none. The second time she was falling backward. Again, no impact.

"That's got to be it: falling. Both times I was falling." She looked at Brian.

He immediately flopped forward onto the ground holding the sprig in front of him. He hit the brown grass with a thud.

"Ah! That kind of hurt," he mumbled.

"Going without me, huh?" She jumped to her feet. "That's it! It's me! Me and falling." She grabbed the sprig from his hand. He leapt to his feet as she was propelling herself on to the ground. He managed to grab her other hand in the nick of time and they both disappeared.

All sound stopped briefly before she found herself lying face down in the dirt behind the 1889 post office. Brian was beside her, holding her hand, also face down.

"Did you both trip, then? Good heavens. Mr. Everbright! Are you all right?" A postal clerk rushed to them and helped Lily to her feet. She brushed the dirt from her dress while the clerk was fussing over Brian. She was back in her 1889 body, like a trusty horse that runs up when you whistle.

Brian was his dapper self, complete with hair crème and a bit of dirt.

"Please sir! Thank you for your assistance but you can now let me be." Clearly agitated, Brian pushed the man back from him. He looked at Lily and gave a sigh of relief. He tugged on his jacket to straighten his clothes.

"Glad to see you are you again," he said.

"Oh! I thought perhaps you were relieved that I was safe. What was I thinking? You're just happy your world is in order."

After the clerk was out of earshot, he took her by the elbow firmly and hissed in her ear. "Dearest Lily, for all I know now, the real you could be that hideous girl with hair like a drowned cat. Of course I'm relieved to see you this way. You should be glad, too. If I have no desire for you, it could go poorly for you and the whole Black family. Yes. Now I know all I need to."

"Let me go!"

"Tell me, does that rough-as-a-cob hillbilly know the truth about you? That could be shocking for him. Or, perhaps that is why he stormed off a bit ago. He knows and he can't stomach it."

That hit a bit too close to home and she winced. "You really are too much, Brian. I'm going home now and honestly, I just want you to leave me alone."

"Go on, then. You are truly a stupid girl. But, don't think this is the end of it." He grabbed her wrist and pulled her close enough for her to feel the heat of his leg through her dress. He leaned in close to her ear as she struggled. "You still make me burn for you. That hasn't changed."

She wriggled free and darted between the post office and the inn back toward Main Street and ran all the way to Black's Farm.

Chapter 10 – The Tree of Life

In the safety of her room upstairs, Lily just wanted to hide under the covers. So much had happened. Still reeling from the trip to Lexington, she had so much passion to move forward with her plans for the girls at the school. Then, Evan stepped in and crushed her spirit with his doubts about her. Now, this bizarre jaunt back to 2018 with Brian had shown her hand to him and also answered many questions about how it all happened.

She tried to breath deep and take her thoughts one at a time. She needed to think of a way to get through to the town council and the parents. The problem was that many of the parents could not read either. They may have been taught to read by a family member, but likely, many of the farmers were pulled to the fields at an early age. It would be hard to convince them that their daughters needed more education than they had.

Farming was changing, though. She'd heard William talk about it in Versailles. The railroads were allowing investors from far away to move goods into farming markets and creating competition. The Southern Alliance of Farmers was gaining strength. They were networking to save farming as a business. William told Bettie about a meeting they were going to have in Hardinsburg. If she could teach the girls to read the newspaper, they could read it to their fathers when news about the Alliance was reported. This would help the men know what was going on. All the girls would have to do is read it out loud, not necessarily understand it. Of, course in time they would, but for now, it would be a help to the farmers to have the information. She decided that was what she would do. She would teach the girls to read the newspaper and scan for articles about the Alliance.

She breathed a sigh of resolution. Now, she really just wanted to see Evan and have him hold her. She wanted to feel his arms around her and hear his voice in her ear. She got up from the bed and went to the window. It was getting dark and she could see firelight from his cottage window across the field. He was in there.

She hastened to slip down the stairs and out the front door. William and Bettie were talking in the kitchen. She slipped around the house and made her way across the field. On the porch of the farmhand's cottage, she peered in the bubbled glass window to see what he was doing.

His back was to her as he sat in a rocking chair in front of the fire. She decided to knock. There was a long silent pause. She wondered if he had peeked through the window to see who was there before deciding to open the door. Finally, the door slowly opened.

"You need to go back to the main house, Lily. It's not right that you should be here."

"I can't help it. I miss you, Evan. It was so long in Lexington and I missed you. Please don't push me away. We can figure this out together."

He sighed and stepped out onto the small porch. The sky was already dark and Lily, turning her head to look, could see movement in Bettie's kitchen through the lighted

213

windows. William sat at the table smoking a pipe. The field was dark now.

Before she turned back, Evan scooped her into his arms and pulled her close. The warmth of his embrace made her melt.

"Oh, Evan. You feel like home."

"You do, too, Lily. I have thought about it all afternoon and there isn't any logical answer to what's happening, but I know what my heart feels. I tried to run from it once before and it was no good. I know better now."

He briefly looked into her eyes before giving up any fears he had. Then he kissed her softly at first, and then with a passion that comes from a heart overflowing with want. He didn't just want her body, he wanted the spirit inside her body to be with him always.

Time, culture, career, birthplace or birthright, none of it mattered. He clearly saw now that no matter what skin she had or what were her goals for her life, he wanted to be beside her. He wanted to love her and be loved.

In a breathless moment as he kissed her face she whispered. "I know what caused the time travel to happen."

He stopped suddenly and looked at her.

"Well, maybe not what caused it, but how it works, anyway."

"What are you trying to say?"

"When you left me earlier, Brian approached me. We had a tussle."

"What? That scoundrel! I'll kill him." He looked past her into the darkness as though Brian might be there.

She held him in his seat by his hands. "No! Wait. Let me finish."

He stopped trying to get up and listened.

"We lost our balance and fell to the ground, but not before I managed to grab a sprig of cedar trying to slow the fall. Well, we never actually hit the ground and the next thing I knew I was in 2018 with Brian."

"What?" This time he did stand up looking at me with wide eyes.

She stood, too. "We were in different bodies. Teenagers." She snorted, "It was kind of funny, really."

"I see nothing funny about this. You were over a hundred years away from me. With him. How is that funny?"

"Maybe you had to be there. But anyway, it was the cedar sprig, and me, and falling. All three of those facts together, makes me time travel."

"So how did he go with you? And are you sure it's just you?"

"He was touching me, so he went. He tried without me, to get back, and it didn't work. I actually tried to leave him there in the future but he managed to grab my hand and came back with me."

"So he knows all this about you now."

"Yes. It doesn't matter. What's he going to do with that information? No one would believe him."

"I'm not sure, but I surely don't trust him." He paused looking away.

"Evan, what is it?"

He turned back to her. "You came back to me. To 1889. Why? You could have just stayed there. You'd found a way home."

"Yes and no. It was a way home, but I wasn't me. I don't know why my body didn't show up. Why was I in the teenage body? My car was gone. Maybe I drowned in the creek in the future. I don't know. I could have stayed but I was in another body. No one would have recognized me.

215

And besides, you are here. I want to marry you. I want to change education one kid at a time. This is a great place to make differences that will last for centuries. Public education is forming right now, in this time."

"True, but being in a different body can't be any worse than me pulling you up a muddy creek back into 1889?"

"I know. I just had to get back. I was worried it wouldn't work again. What if there are only so many times it will work or if the stars have to be in the right place. I just had to try. Immediately."

He kissed her lightly again. "You make me very happy. Lily Wallingsford, I shall never care what body you are in. It's your heart I love."

She smiled. "I feel the same for you, Evan. I had purple hair, though!" She snorted. "Would you love me with purple hair?"

"Yes. I would love you with any hair." He sat on the bench pulling her down to sit with him again. "Lily, I want you to be my wife. Soon. We need to settle this matter. Maybe then, he will leave you alone."

The cool spring air wafted over them giving her chills. A storm was brewing overhead and rumblings of thunder were coming from downriver. Suddenly Lily smelled the sweet scent of water in the air. Rain was close.

"I want that, too, Evan."

"Now that I have land, we can build our house and start a family. There is so much to do. Let's just move on and forget him."

"Okay. You're right."

"Let's marry this Saturday. Here at Black's farm." He decided.

"This weekend? I'll need Bettie's help. I don't know what to do to get ready."

216

He smiled. "I know she will help. She loves you already. Anything you need, just put it on my account. I want you to have the wedding of which you have always dreamed."

He kissed her softly and she got lost in the wave of love she felt. She could have melted in his arms right then. He held her tightly and exhaled. A sense of relief filled her. She looked up toward the heavens and the shifting clouds opened a window to the stars. The galaxy peeked in on her and the stars seemed to wink.

Evan took her by the hand and led her out into the moonlight. By the sounds of the loud cicadas' raspy song, he held her against him and danced a waltz in whirling circles. Her gown flung out around her as they swirled on the new spring grass. The soft breeze ruffled her hair and goosebumps rose on the back of her neck.

Evan leaned down and pressed his cheek against hers. The day's growth of stubble tickled her senses even further. She closed her eyes and let him lead her in the dance, taking in the scent of rain, the scratch of his cheek, the katydid rubbing like a metal zipper, and the heat of his body next to her. She had never felt more alive or more whole.

He slowly stopped and pulled her tighter with his arms around her. "Lily, I don't know what magic brought you to me, but I'm grateful. I couldn't imagine living without you."

***

Brian stood at the window of his clothing store watching the people walk past outside. He looked down the street and could easily count twenty individuals. How many more were inside stores? In the future, he'd only seen two people. A crotchety old man and a postal clerk. No stores, no

217

sternwheelers docking and unloading, not even a passenger train.

"There is no future in this town," he mumbled to himself.

"What's that you say?" his father asked.

"Oh, father! I didn't see you. I was just wondering about the future of this town."

"I'd say Stephensport is on a grand path! It'll be the largest town between Louisville and Owensboro. Just look, son. Can't you see it?" He pointed out the window at the people milling in the street.

"Perhaps, father. But what if something changes. What if we didn't have the railroad bringing people and the sternwheelers loading coal and crops here?"

"I suppose that would be awful. Our family has invested heavily in this town buying property and even sponsoring the building of the rail station itself. If this town dries up, we would be bankrupt. But, listen son, this town belongs to the merchants and the businesses. Nothing is going to change that."

Brian nodded, his face went pale. His father walked back to the counter and began putting new merchandise into the glass case.

Brian's face turned downward as he looked back out at the street. "Everything we have we have put into this town. All our eggs are in one basket."

A boy with a cotton sack crossed over his shoulder opened the door to the shop and handed Brian the morning paper before turning and darting back out. Brian scanned the headlines of the Courier Journal. His eyes caught on a particular story and he froze.

***

218

Lily and Bettie sat at the table in the kitchen finishing breakfast. Lily had been quiet and Bettie started peering at her between bites.

"Darlin', you have something on your mind. Now what is it?" Bettie asked.

Lily looked up. "Oh! I'm just thinking about lesson plans."

"Lesson plans? Well how hard is that? You do some reading and you do some arithmetic and call it a day. Nothing to trouble your head with there."

Lily laughed. "I know it seems like it should be no big deal, but a lot of thought actually goes into a good lesson plan." Then she added, "If you want it to actually be a good lesson."

"Huh." Bettie just looked at her. Lily could tell Bettie had no idea.

"It's okay. I just want to make some changes and I am trying to play it out in my mind ahead of time."

"Changes? Well I hope you are seeing a bunch of people with torches and pitchforks in that scene in your head. Change doesn't go well around here. I mean, I know in my lifetime, this town has changed some. The railroad coming through has made a big difference. More stores and banks are here. But, most of the people that live here date back to the war. And I don't mean the war between the states. They have a heritage that runs deep for many generations. Their families have been farmers for so long, the ground probably could tell you what should be planted when. It's worked for them for a long time and change isn't part of their heritage."

Lily listened to her speak and the clarity of her statement gave her chills. She was right. The farmers eventually win out. Lily already knew how this story would end. In fact, she herself was a product of it. Eventually Bettie's very own

219

great granddaughter would move away so they could find work in Louisville. She herself would be born in Frankfort and would never grow up in Stephensport because life here would be harder than life in a bigger town.

"You're probably right about that, Bettie. But still, maybe education can make things better for those people. Maybe it will help them be able to fight for the rights of farmers."

"Now, that is good thinking." Bettie smiled.

Lily excused herself, picked up her lunch pail, and set off for the schoolhouse. She decided Bettie was right. She could frame her purpose for teaching the girls to read in such a way that it would be helpful for the farmers. If women could read and converse about topics affecting farming, and write letters to state legislators, men would have more time to just get the farming done. As she walked through town, she stopped at the dry goods store and picked up a copy of the Courier Journal, Louisville's newspaper, to take to school for reading material. She tucked it into her apron pocket.

She climbed the stairs to the school, inserted the old skeleton key into the lock and stepped inside. The room was dark and her eyes were accustomed to the morning sunlight. She closed the door behind her and felt the impact of a man hitting her side with such force she was knocked off her feet.

All sound stopped. Darkness surrounded her. All she could feel was a man's arms around her. Seconds passed and she realized she was on the ground.

"Get off me!" she yelled as she tried to pry his arms off her.

"Certainly, my dear. Let me help you up. I apologize for having to clobber you that way. I assumed you would not come willingly."

Her eyes adjusted to the darkness and she could see Brian's stiff postured frame more clearly. "What's wrong with you? Can't you just leave me alone?"

"I will now. You have served your purpose." He threw the sprig of cedar on the floor.

"What are you talk--" she broke off as she scanned the walls. She wasn't in the school room. It appeared to be a vacant church built in the 1960s. Indoor/outdoor carpet, pews with worn green upholstery, and a large smooth wood cross on the front wall. The tips of the cross taper down to points on the ends. This was definitely not 1889. From the looks of the room, she had no idea what decade this was.

She looked down and saw the same skinny jeans as their last trip forward. She reached up and felt crunchy spikey short hair. One look at him now that her eyes adjusted and she could see, and she knew they were back in 2018.

She jumped down to the floor and snatched up the sprig. Holding it close, she crouched and backed away from him.

"Heavens. I'm not going to try to take it. You can stop guarding it. I told you. I got what I wanted."

Seeing that he wasn't moving toward her, she stood upright. She held the sprig tightly in her hand and flung herself into the air. For just a moment, she believed it would happen, that sound would leave and the space around her grow dark, and then she would be in Evan's world again.

With a loud thump, she hit the floor. First her crossed arms hit, crushed beneath her. Then her forehead made contact and she slid a few inches across the worn carpet.

She opened her eyes and slowly looked up. The long-since forgotten church still surrounded her. The smell of mildew in the carpet tickled her nose. She pushed herself up off the floor and turned to see Brian watching with his arms crossed and a hand on his chin.

"Fascinating. I suppose there was actually a limit. No harm no fowl. You're back where you started and haven't lost anything."

"No harm, no foul?" she yelled. "Yes, there was harm and foul. I didn't want to come back. I had a better life there. Now you stole that!"

"What? You lost a future as a farmer's wife? You would have worn yourself out having a dozen babies, likely dying in childbirth. And if not that, you would have had a lifetime of hardship and toil. Honestly, is that what life is now?" He waved his hand in the air.

"Wow. You may be right that my life would have been a lot of work back there, but you may be surprised how hard, and lonely, it is in the future."

She shoved her hand down into her pocket. The money was there. "Well, at least this time, I have cab fare."

She turned and went to the front door. He just stood there thinking.

"So what is your big plan? Apparently you have a plan."

He looked up at her, "Actually, it was an impulse. I realized that staying in 1889 would lead to my ruin."

"So you just thought you'd ruin my life by using me as a magic bus to the future? You're a real trip. Good luck, Brian Everbright." She turned the lock and was out the door. She ran to the post office across the street.

Breathing hard, she burst in the door.

"Yeah, girly. You got another letter? The last one hasn't even gone out yet," the clerk said. He was a tired looking fella. His skin was kind of pale and wrinkled.

"Uh, no. I need a cab. Can you call me a cab? How much do you think a cab to Frankfort would cost?"

222

"Frankfort! Good Lord, girl. That's two, maybe three, hours away. I have no idea how much that would cost, but I'll call you a cab."

"Okay. Thanks. And hey, what's the date?"

He stopped dialing and pointed to an office wall calendar with a pencil. The eraser tapped on the white square that had a big '2' in the corner. She saw that it said January 2018 across the top. When she nodded slowly, he turned back to the phone and started talking to someone at the cab dispatch.

The clerk hung up the phone and turned to her. "Okay, honey. You can wait outside on the bench. They will be right over. It's just old Henry. He's a one-man cab service. He said he would take you there."

"Thank you."

"Good luck to ya," he called after her.

She sat on the bench and tried to make sense of it all. She realized that if this was the same day, wouldn't she be in Frankfort right now or would she be passing by soon? She hadn't checked the time. Maybe she had already passed by and her old self was up at the cemetery. Time was bending on itself. Soon, the old Lily would careen off the bridge and be gone, back to 1889 and the loop would continue.

Before long an old silver car pulled up with a magnetic sticker on the door. It said 'Henry's Cab'. She opened the back door and got in. Before she could close the door, the other door opened and a teenager in a Monster shirt jumped in with her. It took her a minute to realize it was Brian, but when he straightened stiffly and tugged down on his tee shirt, she knew it was him.

"Hey, you got the money? You're gonna have to pay some in advance to go that far."

"Sure." She pulled the two twenties out of her pocket and handed them over.

223

"Okay then, off we go." The driver pulled out and headed toward the gray structure of the bridge over Sinking Creek.

Brian's eyes widened as he looked out the window. His head swiveled back and forth as he tried to look at houses they passed. He grabbed his stomach and turned pale.

She just shook her head and whispered. "So what are you doing coming with me? You might have had some authority in your time, but you can forget it now. You are not following me around forever."

"That's not very courteous. I see myself as a guest in your time."

"Courteous? Are you kidding me? How courteous have you been to me? You assaulted me this morning. Oh, and I know what you tried to do to Evan."

Henry's eyes darted at her through the mirror. She gave him a nod and curt smile to convey she was okay. He turned his attention back to the road.

"What do they say? Old news? I think that's fitting given the current year."

"Maybe, but I know and that's all that matters."

The country side looked so much the same. Other than the occasional brick home, hibernating farmland filled with shreds of last year's stalks or pastures dotted with a few cows could have been from any time. They crossed through hamlet of Union Star and she caught a glimpse of the full cemetery. Some of her own family was in there. She realized that many from 1889 were in there. It occurred to her, not far from here, this very minute, there was a small church with a cemetery and Bettie and William were there.

Her heart lurched and crumpled. She missed Bettie already. If Bettie and William were gone, then so was Evan. She tried desperately to block the thought of him lying in the ground just bones and dust now.

She turned and gazed out the window in the direction of the old church. She could barely hear it at first, but it grew louder. A hollow moan that seemed to come from the air itself. She knew it was the call of whatever had sent her through time. Perhaps it was her grandmother's ghost or even more ancient ancestors.

She glanced at Brian. He looked ridiculous in his skinny jeans and Converse sneakers sitting bolt upright with his shoulders back like the king of England on parade, hands clasped over his knee. He didn't say anything as he stared out the window. He didn't seem to hear the ever increasing tone.

It got louder until she put her hands over her ears. Brian look at her curiously.

"Can't you hear it?" she yelled.

"Hear what? You don't have to yell." He looked concerned now with a furrowed brow.

She fainted back into the seat. The last thing she heard was Brian calling her name as he slapped her.

***

Dizziness washed over her. She was now standing in the living room of her apartment. She looked down and she was her old self. She wasn't in the cab. She wasn't the teenager. She was back in her own body. Andrew was gone. She dashed to the window to see if he was still there in his car.

Andrew was gone, but there was the gardener. He turned then and looked at her. She jumped back. A strange feeling came over her, like she knew the gardener. He was not a random groundskeeper. Something about him was familiar. She pulled the curtain back again. This time he was at her door about to knock.

She dashed to the door and opened it. For just a moment they stared into each other's eyes.

"Evan?" she whispered tilting her head.

A smile broke out that lit his whole face. It was not his skin or eyes, but the spirit of Evan shined through.

"Lily, my love. Are you in there?"

"Yes, it's me. I was," she wracked her brain trying to figure it out. "I was in a cab. With Brian. We were in the teenagers' bodies. Then, I just passed out and I was standing here. In my body. I don't know how. Maybe the other me in this time crashed over the bridge at that moment."

She scrunched her eyebrows. "This is crazy, isn't it? But, but how are you here?"

"Apparently it's not just you, my darling. I grabbed me a sprig of cedar and took a flying leap off the porch, right in front of Bettie and with her blessing. She may have just wanted to make fun of me in case I fell face down on the ground."

She laughed at that.

"The school kids sent a messenger that ye weren't in the school house but your turned-over lunch pail and newspaper were on the floor. It had the look of something bad. I dashed to the clothiers and saw that Brian was nowhere to be found and knew something was wrong. I had to try something."

She threw her arms around him. "Oh, Evan! Oh my goodness. You're alive!"

"I surely hope so."

"It's just, they're all gone now. It's been a century." A tear formed in the corner of her eye.

"My Lily, do not fash yerself about the past or the confines of a lifetime. Our love for each other and the people we've shared life with, its all in here." He pointed to his heart.

226

"So what are we going to do? We could just go back. Let's just go back now. You probably have more times to travel left. Apparently I have maxed out my travel ticket, but we could go together."

He was quiet for a moment. "Lily, are ye sure? We are here together. I have all I need. This is yer time. Ye even have your own body, which I happen to find quite enticing."

He slipped his arm around her waist. "I'm not sure what you're wearing--,"

"These are called leggings and this is a tank top," she interrupted pointing as she spoke.

He continued, "But, if all women of this time wear them, it must be wonderful. All the women run around in their bloomers?"

She giggled. "They are fairly normal clothes."

He kissed her neck and growled.

"Okay, okay. I'm glad to know that I don't have to be twenty and drop-dead gorgeous for you to want me. But seriously, we need to decide what we are going to do."

He pulled himself away from her neck and looked around her apartment. "Is this where ye live? It's so rich. Yer rug covers that whole floor." He glanced at the kitchen. "And the kitchen, it looks so, so different. Can ye have a fire in that stove? What is that tall metal cabinet?"

"Just wait until you see!" She dashed into the kitchen and opened the refrigerator. "Ta da! It keeps everything cold." She slammed it shut and opened the freezer. "Or frozen." Slamming that shut, she pushed on the ice dispenser in the door and ice cubes fell onto her outstretched hand and onto the floor with a crunch.

"What in the world is this magic?" He stepped forward and picked up a piece of ice on the floor.

"No magic, sweetheart. Just modern ingenuity. Are you hungry? I'll make you a frozen pizza."

"Frozen what? I don't think frozen food would taste good."

She laughed. "Very funny. It will be hot and steamy when it's ready. Watch!" She opened the freezer and pulled out a single-serve pizza in a box. She tore open the side and flipped the lid underneath to make a silver platform and tore the plastic off the pizza.

He picked up the plastic on the counter and held it up to the light. Droplets of water dripped onto his hand.

She put the small circle of pizza on top of the box and opened the microwave. He watched with great interest. She pushed several beeping buttons and the microwave lit up and started to hum. The pizza moved in a circle inside.

"This is incredible." He was transfixed. The cheese soon started to bubble and the pepperoni crackled. "I can smell it! It smells wonderful."

The microwave dinged and she took it out. He tried to touch it and pulled his hand away fast. "It's so hot, but it only cooked for a minute!"

"Actually two minutes and thirty seconds, but yes, it is very hot. I'll put it on a plate."

She put it on a plate and cut it into four slices with a pizza cutter. "Here. Sit down." She took the plate to her small kitchen table and motioned for him to sit down.

He looked at her and she nodded. He picked up a piece and timidly nibbled at the edge. "Oh! My darling. Ye're the greatest cook I have ever met."

"Thanks, but I can't really take the credit. Stouffers actually made it. I just heated it."

"Is this how all food is made?"

228

"Oh, no. You can still cook the old fashioned way. No one has time, though. This is convenience food. I'm too tired to cook when I get home from work."

He ate the entire pizza in a few bites and brushed the crumbs off his fingers. "Too tired to cook? That's terrible. Although, this 'convincing food' is not bad."

"Con-veen-yence food. It's convenient. Here. Let me get you some water." She went back to the fridge and got a bottled water.

He looked at it and then looked at the sink. "Thank you. Does the water pump not work?"

She laughed. "Oh, yeah. It works fine. But this is cold and tastes better."

He unscrewed the cap and took a drink. "It does taste fine. Can I try the pump? I'm curious."

"Sure!" She jumped up to watch. He turned the lever on the side of the tall faucet.

"Ouch! It's hot!" he exclaimed as his put his hand under the stream.

"Are you okay? Turn it this way for cold." She turned the lever upwards. "See. Now its cold."

"It makes hot and cold water? This is incredible." He lifted his cupped hand to his mouth. "It tastes fine to me."

"It's okay. It's just easier in the bottle. I can take it with me in the car."

"Yes, your kargh. Ye have talked about that. Is that what those large machines are outside?"

"Yes. I suppose they are like wagons that don't need horses."

"Fascinating." He walked back into the living room and sat on the sofa. "Ye have so much to make life easier now, but yet ye have no time to cook even simple meals. It must be terribly difficult to live in this time that even with all these conveniences you are tired."

She sat down beside him, tucking one leg under her bottom. "I will admit, 1889 is a simpler time. It's not as complicated. Hard work actually pays off. Sometimes in this time you can work yourself to death and end up with nothing."

"So ye would leave all this? Hot and cold water magically pouring out in your kitchen, ice cubes jumping into your hands, and a whole meal ready in a minute?"

She looked into his eyes and yearned to live his life. "Yes. I have no idea how to be a housewife in your time, but I can learn. Bettie can teach me, if you can be patient. As long as you don't mind me teaching, too."

He ran his fingers through her short bob hairstyle that flipped out at the ends. "Yer hair looks as though it was caught in a mill accident."

"Well, thank you, I guess?" She laughed.

"It's just so wild. I like it. You would look very odd walking down Main Street, though."

"I'm sure. Good thing my body in 1889 has more appropriate hair!"

"As good as it is here, I am more comfortable in my own time. It seems so scattered and ineffective here, from what you say. At least I know with my farm, I can grow food and feed my family. My destiny is mine to make from the sweat of my brow."

She nodded. "So let's go. Do you have the cedar twig?"

"But, darling, I don't care what the date is. I just want to be with ye. I can learn to live in this time."

"I appreciate that. I really do, but I want to live in your time. I never thought I would like living in the 'good ol' days,' but I feel more normal then than I do now. So you have the cedar sprig?"

He thought for a moment. "Yes. It's outside." He got up and strode across the room to the door. She stood up and looked around. She had no idea if her body would return here or if she would never be heard from again. Her parents would get her letter explaining as best she could.

She considered taking a picture of them, but it seemed that objects didn't travel well. She gave her apartment one last look and closed the locked door behind her.

She heard a cracking sound and spun around. Brian in his teenage body had just sucker punched Evan from the side. Evan's gardener body was much more mature than the teenager, so he recovered quickly and stood up.

"Brian! How did you get here?" she yelled as she ran to them.

Evan looked stunned. He pointed at Brian and asked, "This is Brian? You have to be kidding." He threw back his head and laughed loudly. Brian came at him again and Evan just held him back with his left hand on Brian's forehead.

"What a delightful turn of events. This will be good. This is for trying to have me killed." Evan balled up his right fist and cocked it back. He hit Brian square on the nose so hard Lily felt an immediate wave of nausea. Brian spun around and landed face down in the grass.

Lily ran to Evan. "Where is the cedar twig?"

Evan saw it by a bush and grabbed it.

"Please grandma, let the cedar sprig work one more time." Lily thought of her grandmother, knowing she had to have been the one to orchestrate this twist of fate. Surely her grandmother was watching over her even now.

He put his arm around her waist and the two of them leapt forward.

Chapter 11 – Beginning a New Life

"That was very satisfying," Evan mumbled as he rolled over in the grass.

Lily rolled the other way. The crystal blue sky was dotted with puffy clouds. She heard the chugging of the steam engine rolling into Stephensport Station. A plume of steam was wafting over town disappearing into thin air.

She looked at Evan, her strong, gorgeous Scotsman. He smiled the same smile no matter what body he was in. Her long blond hair was coming out of the bun. She sat up and tried to redo it.

He pulled her back down and rolled against her. "Yer hair looks a mess but at least ye didn't catch it in a mill!" He bent down to her lips and kissed her.

She held her breath as the zing of emotion razed through her core. The warmth of his body next to her made her feel like she was home. Home in front of a cozy fire on the coldest night. She was home.

Evan propped up on his elbow and smiled. "So how do ye think he will fair in the future?"

"He'll fit right in with all the other opportunists. He'll find a way. He wanted to be there. That's why he jumped me this morning at the school. He needed me to carry him there."

232

"I'm surprised that he gave up everything he had here."

"It doesn't make sense. Honestly, I'm just glad he's gone," she said.

"That makes two of us."

She sat up and repined her hair. "I really need to get to the school. I'm sure the kids went home but I have plans to make."

He scooted next to her and took her hand in his. "My love, do whatever ye need to. I cannot wait until Saturday when I will call ye my wife." He kissed her tenderly and smiled.

They walked back to town together and parted ways when they got to Black's Farm. She opened the door to the school house and found all her students inside. They were huddled in pairs of a boy with each girl. Each pair had a section of the newspaper and the boy was trying to help the girl sound out words. Lily's eyes stung and began to tear.

"Children, what are you doing?"

Joseph stood up, "Mrs. Wallingsford! You're safe!"

"Yes, Joseph. Thank you for your concern. And, for alerting Mr. McEwen. He saved me. But, what are you all doing with the newspaper? How could you have known I would use it for the lesson today?"

"Well, ma'am, I saw the article about the alliance and read some of it out loud. The girls listened and wanted to know about it. They said if they could read and the boys couldn't, that they would read it to us. We just figured we would show 'em how to read so they could read it themselves."

Lily clasped her hands under her chin. "You children are brilliant. You don't even need me to lead you! That's exactly what I hoped would come about. It won't be easy or quick, but yes, we can teach the girls to read and they will be an asset to their families."

The children all jumped up and surrounded her.

"I'm so proud of you. Let's get to work. Take your seats and we will start at the beginning with the girls, but you boys can be instrumental in making the process move faster. You've really shown great courage and strength by your actions today. You are truly men and women of the future!"

***

Evan stepped into the house and Bettie hollered, "William? Is that you?"

"No, ma'am, it's Evan." He hung his hat on the hat hook by the door.

Bettie bustled in and put her hands on his arms. "It didn't work, then."

"To the contrary! Ye would not believe the marvelous things I have seen, Bettie!"

"But what about Lily?"

"Lily is just fine. We came back together and she went on to the school for a bit."

Bettie clutched her heart and gave a loud sigh. "Thank the good Lord above."

Evan smiled and turned his face upward. "Aye, thank the good Lord." He looked back at Bettie. "And thank ye for believing in me. She was telling the truth. I traveled to the future. It's a magical place where hot bath water pours from the pump and food cooks itself in a box. Lily lives in luxury."

"Good gracious! And yet you two came back here? Whatever for?"

234

"She tells me despite all the luxury, it's a defeating time. It was her choice to return."

"How unfortunate that the future is not better. However, I am ever so glad to have you both back. I would have missed you terribly."

"And she missed ye. She grieved for ye, Bettie."

"Aw. Sweet child."

"Oh, and ladies wear their bloomers out in public there!"

"Well, I'll be! That's probably the root of all their problems, right there."

"Bettie, I told you before I went to the future that we are hoping to marry on Saturday. Can ye help her prepare. She has no one else."

"You bet! I'll get on it. Oh, I need to send a telegram. If I write it out, would you take it to the telegraph office?"

"Anything ye wish!"

She went to her desk and opened a small box with stationary inside. She wrote a quick note and handed it to Evan. "Hold on while I get you a few pennies from William's office."

***

The children placed the newspaper pages on her desk and filed to their seats. She set the boys to work on an arithmetic assignment and worked with the girls reading a primer in a sort of guided reading format that she would have used with her students in the future. An energy filled them all that could be seen in their determination. The girls tried as hard as they could, cheering each other on. The boys worked with new purpose to succeed, not just for their own good, but for the good of the whole school.

After they had put in a good day of study, the children packed up their lunch pails and headed home with cheerful chatter. Lily tried to put the newspaper back into some kind of order. The tiny print with very few pictures made for a very different cover page than she was used to. She scanned the headlines and her eyes landed on one that made her suck in a breath.

'Granite State Sunk Because of Kentucky Businessman'

Lily quickly read the short article. The men in custody had named a Kentucky man but police weren't releasing any information until he was apprehended.

"So that's why he had to get away. He was on the run." Lily let the paper fall on the desk. "Oh, Brian, your need to control everything finally got you in deeper than you could get out."

She imagined the awkward teenager walking down a side walk in the future. He had no money, no home, and was clueless about the world there. At least he wasn't in jail. Then she thought for a minute, "But, that's what he deserved!"

***

Saturday morning came with a clear spring sunrise and birds singing in the trees. Lily wished her mother was here. On the other hand, she wasn't sure if her mother would be happy for her or not marrying a farmer and facing a life of hard work and very little medical care. Surely she would be happy that Lily had found the desire of her heart.

The door opened wide and Bettie came in with a tray of breakfast. "Rise and shine, beautiful bride!"

"Oh! Bettie! How nice of you!"

236

"This may be the last day you get such treatment, so enjoy it! Today is your day!"

"Oh, Bettie, how will I manage? Will you coach me about what to do?"

"Well, William and I were talking. It'll be a few months before Evan can get a decent house built. You and he can share this room until then and you and I can work on things together. That'll give you a good start."

"That would be awesome!"

"Awesome? Hm. I suppose so. Strange way to put it."

Lily laughed.

"Now Evan told me about the pump in your kitchen that pours out hot bath water. That would be nice, but I'm going to have to go heat you some bath water. A nice hot bath will calm your wedding nerves."

"Thank you, Bettie. You're the best."

"Oh, darlin, you're family and I'm so happy for you and Evan. And by the way, Everleigh and Malcolm will be here today. And, her mother Emory, too."

"Really?" she said as she smiled.

"Certainly! Now eat your breakfast. There's so much to do."

Bettie jumped up and headed out the bedroom door.

Later that morning, Bettie did her hair in a Gibson girl swoop and powdered her face. There was a knock at the door.

"Bettie? Lily? It's me Everleigh. Can I come in?" They heard her voice through the door.

"Oh, yes! Do come in!" called Bettie.

The door opened and Everleigh sashayed in holding a large box.

"Everleigh! I'm so glad you are here!" said Lily.

237

"Well, sure, sweetie! We are a kind of sister that is a very limited sorority. So, what kind of wedding dress have you got?"

Lily looked at Bettie. Bettie said, "There wasn't much time, deary. She is going to wear my best dress that has been altered a little."

"That's kind of what I thought. So I brought this. Now, you can wear whatever you want, but I wanted to show you this. Mother had this gown made for me for my wedding. It's amazing. Would you like to see it?"

"Would I? I'd love to!" said Lily.

Lily could hardly speak looking at all the lace and ruffles of the handmade gown. "This is exquisite! Are you sure you don't mind?"

"I would be honored, girlfriend!"

Lily hugged her. "Thank you so much!" She couldn't help shedding a tear from the wash of love she felt.

"Lily, I do have a request, though."

"Anything!"

"Maybe this summer when school is out, could you come to my place for a couple of weeks and help me with a curriculum for my students? We are doing okay, but I really think that you could help us offer the best program possible for my students."

"I would love that! Yes, yes, yes!"

"Great! Okay, let's getting this wedding going! I know there is a groom around here that's got to be pawing at the ground like a stallion."

***

Lily and Evan were married at Black's Farm next to Sinking Creek with friends and family on a perfect spring day. Everleigh cried tears of joy seeing her gown from a spectator's point of view. All she could think about was her own wonderful wedding and what a fairy tale it had been being with Malcolm

Bettie's gold watch hung around Lily's neck as something new to bring her good luck. Lily chuckled to herself because in her time, this watch was her grandmother's and now passed down to her mother. She smiled thinking that maybe the watch could bring her dear grandmother to this place in time so she could share it with her.

The day was long and joyous. Later that evening after a feast where they all sat in the glorious light of the sunset and talked about the blessing of finding a mate who couldn't live without you, the guest went on their way. The gathering grew smaller and those staying the night decided it was time to settle in.

Finally Lily and Evan were alone in her room, now their room. The moonlight covered the far wall with a peaceful silver glow. Lily wore a pressed cotton nightgown and waited nervously at the vanity, brushing her hair. Awkwardness crept over her as though she had never been alone with him.

Evan slipped out of his trousers and shirtwaist until he was only in his sark. The long linen undershirt covered him as he asked her to join him at the window.

She took a deep breath and stood up. Her steps to the window seemed robotic. When she got within arm's reach, he took her hands in his and pulled her close. The heat of his body radiated through the fabric and the boundary between them blurred. All fear and awkwardness left her as she melted against him. His warm breath caressed her cheek.

"My love, surely I am the happiest man alive. I canna believe how God has blessed me that I might have yer love."

She rested her head on his chest and smiled. The scent of cedar tickled her nose and she breathed deeply.

"Thank you, grandma," she whispered.

"Grandma?"

"Oh, yes. This all has to be my grandma's doing. She loved with her whole heart and only love and faith could have made this miracle."

"Then I shall be forever in yer grandmother's debt."

"Well, oddly, if we live long enough, we could possibly meet her as an infant in about twenty years."

"I will surely call that day blessed."

He wrapped his arms around her waist and held her tightly. As she looked up into his soulful eyes, she felt the room spin. He kissed her, slowly at first, and then with a fierceness. She had never felt so loved by a man. A love expressed merely by his tender, yet hungry touch. She knew it as well as she knew anything: This man would love her all the days of her life and she would love him back.

Lily heard a distant sound like a horn or the vibration of a wet finger encircling the rim of a glass. It was so faint that she knew Evan didn't hear it. It stopped and then the quiet sound of her grandmother's laughter echoed in the wind as it buffeted the glass window.

The End

Epilogue

August 24, 1889

Just before dawn on the day Young's High Bridge in Lawrenceburg celebrated its grand opening, a flash of light was seen on the tracks on the Versailles side.

It wasn't a reflection. It was a burst of energy created when a person manages to cross the timeline in a way that is forced. Brian, in his teenage body from the future, jumped out of an ellipse of light and fell onto the tracks. His clothes were rags and anyone would have taken him for being homeless. His dirty tight blue jeans and ripped tee shirt made him look like a runaway from the future.

He stumbled over a railroad tie and lost his balance. Falling between the open beams, his leg twisted and broke with a crack. His breathing quickened as the searing pain radiating from his femur. He was wedged in a crevice between the metal and wood in such a way that he could not see anything but straight down to the Kentucky River or straight up to the metal rails about a foot beyond his reach.

His time in the future, brief as it was, showed him the mistake of running from your problems. He was a nothing in 2018. He'd been run out of stores, cornered by druggies, and chased police. Decent people wouldn't talk to him and the only job prospect he could find was working at Taco Bell. He managed to endure one hour of making tacos before he told them all he was not meant for this kind of life and ran for the door.

Now he was trapped. Sharp agony in his thigh was so overwhelming that he just wanted to let it take him into the oblivion that threatened. Pinpoints of light pricked his vision. He reached into his jeans pocket and pulled out the chain and pocket watch that had helped him time travel. He'd stolen it.

He knew this gold watch from the delicate floral etching. It was the one around Lily's neck the night she'd come to dinner at his house. A woman in Frankfort was wearing it and he couldn't look away from it. He wondered how she had gotten it. Maybe it had been sold to an antique dealer. What he didn't know was that the watch had been Bettie's and the woman wearing it was Bettie's great-great-granddaughter.

In a rush of anger at how his life turned out, he shoved the woman down, took the watch, and ran. He shoved it in his pocket and jumped into the back of a Wild Turkey Bourbon truck just before the door slammed shut. When the truck reached the distillery on the Lawrenceburg side of the bridge and the door was opened, he made a run for it. The truck driver and a security guard gave pursuit. Darting here and there, he found his way to the bridge and started heading across. He could hear sirens in the distance.

That's where pathetic confusion happened. He got to the middle and started sobbing with the rush of adrenaline. Where was he going to go? What difference did it make? This watch and memory of what could have been were all he had of Lily. He was never going to be the aristocrat he was born to be. He shoved his hand in his pocket and felt the watch vibrating a warm radiating heat. He closed his eyes and begged God to release him from his terrible life where no time was his.

The light flashed around him and the distillery disappeared. The bridge seemed brand new. For just a moment, he thought maybe God had answered his prayer for escape, but the deeds of our lives eventually catch up to us. For Brian Everbright, a slow, agonizing, lonely death was his future. He shivered in the cool mist wafting up from the river. Shock was setting in. He pulled the chain around his neck and closed his eyes.

A note from the author: I hope you enjoyed this story. Please leave a review on Amazon and let me and other readers know what you thought of it. You can follow my blog at www.carolynbondwriter.com. I would love to hear from you.

Made in the USA
Columbia, SC
05 November 2018